Chase gave a ha

'If I had a wife,' he
would not have her o̶ . . . o share mine.'

'She'd have to want to,' Sky blurted out. Oh, God, why couldn't she control her tongue?

His green eyes met hers. 'Oh,' he said slowly, meaningfully, 'she'd want to.'

Disturbing images flooded her mind and she pushed them away with an effort. 'Sure of yourself, aren't you?' she asked.

He smiled. 'Oh, very. . .'

Dear Reader

The nights are drawing in again . . . the perfect excuse for snuggling up with a Mills & Boon romance! November is the time for bonfires and fireworks, of course—and you'll find plenty of sparks flying between the heroes and heroines in this month's collection of love stories! Look out for books by some of your favourite authors . . . and, if you're missing the summer sun, why not let us transport you to sunny California and exotic Mexico? So shut out the winter darkness, and enter the warm and wonderful world of Mills & Boon!

The Editor

Ever since **Karen van der Zee** was a child growing up in Holland she wanted to do two things: write books and travel. She's been very lucky. Her American husband's work as a development economist has taken them to many exotic locations. They were married in Kenya, had their first daughter in Ghana and their second in the United States. They spent two fascinating years in Indonesia. Since then they've added a son to the family as well. They now live in Virginia, but not permanently!

Recent titles by the same author:

MAKING MAGIC
A LOVE UNTAMED

CAPTIVE IN EDEN

BY

KAREN VAN DER ZEE

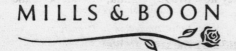

MILLS & BOON LIMITED
ETON HOUSE, 18-24 PARADISE ROAD
RICHMOND, SURREY TW9 1SR

MILLS & BOON and the Rose Device are trademarks of the publisher.

First published in Great Britain 1994 by Mills & Boon Limited

© Karen van der Zee 1994

Australian copyright 1994   Philippine copyright 1994 This edition 1994

ISBN 0 263 78746 X

Set in Times Roman 11 on 12 pt. 01-9411-48914 C

Made and printed in Great Britain

CHAPTER ONE

BY THE time they arrived at the old Virginia plantation house for the cocktail party, Sky was clenching her teeth and her stomach churned. She should have waited to tell Sean the news until later, only she'd been so excited and she'd hoped so much he'd understand and be excited too.

But he wasn't.

She let the anger squash down the pain. Anger was easier to deal with for the moment.

'We'll discuss this later,' he said now as he parked the car. His voice was coldly businesslike and it made her furious. She was not one of his employees who were being paid to do what he told them to. She was her own person with her own life and her own dreams and she had the right to make her own decisions.

He held the car door open for her and she swung her legs to the side and got out, giving his handsome face a stony stare as she did so.

Silently they walked the short way up to the front doors of the plantation house. It was a beautiful historic building with a large wrap-around porch and formally landscaped gardens. It was worth a ton of money, but the owners of the Montana Group had tons of money, according to Sean.

A butler ushered them into a marble-floored foyer and into a large, high-ceilinged room where the cocktail party was in full swing. Men in sober suits and women in elegant dresses stood around in small groups, talking and smiling. Diamonds glittered and champagne flowed. Waiters weaved around with trays of drinks and platters of beautifully presented food.

'There he is,' said Sean. 'The man rubbing his chin.'

The man rubbing his chin looked just as Sky had expected—tall, sophisticated, sleek and ruthless. His dark suit was impeccable, his dress shirt blindingly white, his hair combed back and trimmed immaculately. He had striking green eyes that had a predatory glint in them as he glanced around the room. Looking for prey, she thought with a spark of amusement, the assessment instinctive. Here was a man with power and money, one of the owners of the Montana Group, a family company that owned luxury hotels and tourist resorts the world over. And they were here to celebrate one more project—a large tourist hotel in the Ecuadorian rainforest. She didn't like the sound of it one bit.

The green eyes clashed with hers. An electric spark tingled through her nervous system and her heart missed a beat. No wonder—she didn't like that arrogant self-possession he emanated; it made the hair prickle at the back of her neck. His eyes not leaving her face, he came towards them, moving forward with an economy of movement, weaving through the crowd of people, easily and confidently—a man at home in his own body.

And a good body it was, she had no doubt. Just watching him move told her that.

His smile was polite. 'Sean, glad you could make it,' he said in a deep, utterly masculine voice that had a faint, elegant southern lilt. But his tone was cool, as were his eyes as he looked at Sean.

He doesn't like Sean, she thought, and then the penetrating green gaze was full on her face and he extended his hand to her. 'Chase Montana,' he said, not giving Sean the chance to introduce them.

His hand was firm as he grasped hers. Her heart began to gallop at the look of interest in his eyes. No, not mere interest—it was more intense than that. Perhaps it was only because of the green of his eyes, compelling eyes that missed nothing.

His hair was a rich, dark brown. He had a nose with a bump on it—Roman, or Greek—she wasn't sure what they called it. Or maybe somebody had broken his nose in a rage. She could well imagine such a possibility. He was a man who could evoke extremes of emotion, she was quite sure. Unaccountably, a shiver went down her spine. It was an odd experience to have such an instant, strong reaction to a stranger.

'Sky Malone,' she told him and tried to extract her hand. He was holding on just a bit too long for comfort.

One dark brow arched fractionally. 'Sky...an interesting name. I like it.'

'Thank you,' she said politely. 'So do I.'

His mouth quirked. 'Please, come in and have a drink.'

Sean went straight for the Scotch. Sky kept to a glass of champagne and slipped away from Sean into a small adjoining room where a table in the middle held a miniature version of the hotel and grounds that would be constructed in Ecuador.

Maps, photographs, blueprints and artist renderings were displayed on the walls.

Twenty-five acres of primal rainforest would be cleared for the project. Roads would be built, hiking paths hacked through the jungle, a boating dock built at the river's edge.

Wealthy tourists would flock to the hotel from where they could discover the miracle that was the rainforest, and gawk at the indigenous people living there, who, of course, would gawk back.

Having had a good look around, Sky left the room. Sean was deep in conversation with two other men, smiling and looking animated.

Sean was handsome, charming and smart. She'd liked the charming part of him the best, at least when she'd first met him a few months ago. Lately it was beginning to annoy her. He liked being charming a little too much. The smart part had some problems too, as far as Sky was concerned. She hadn't immediately noticed this, but it had become more and more obvious that Sean was manipulative and controlling, character traits that made her want to run screaming for the woods.

During the drive over to the party, the atmosphere had soured as soon as she had mentioned her trip to Mexico. He had stiffened and waves of disapproval had billowed forth from him.

'A *month*?' he'd said, incredulous.

'Yes.'

'Sky, you can't leave for a whole month. I *need* you.'

This was supposed to make her feel good—loved, wanted.

It made her furious.

She didn't get angry easily and she'd stared rigidly out of the car window trying to stay calm, trying to find the humour in the situation. But Sean was being selfish and it simply wasn't humorous.

She watched him now as he was being his charming self, feeling her heart contract. It was going wrong. Again it was going wrong. Again there was that terrible sense of loneliness at the realisation that she had to do her dreaming and hoping by herself.

With Josh she had shared everything and together they had planned and dreamed. He had thought everything she did with her camera was magic; she'd thought everything he wrote with his pen was magic.

She sighed and took a drink from her champagne. She was twenty-seven years old and she was never, never going to find another man she could love. She was going to end up sad, single and childless—lonely and unfulfilled. She looked down at the bubbly champagne in her glass and grinned at her own melodrama. Sometimes, making fun of her own fears made them easier to face.

Still, eight years was a long time to be alone, a long time to be lonely. None of the other men she had known since Josh had been able to fill up the emptiness. Maybe something was wrong with her. Maybe subconsciously she picked the wrong men, for whatever perverse, hidden reason.

The large French doors stood open and the outside gardens beckoned. The wildlife outside was much more interesting than the wildlife inside, so she slipped out into the cool evening air.

It was a lovely spring night with lots of stars and a half-moon. Discreetly hidden outdoor lights illuminated the gardens, creating a romantic, fairy-tale atmosphere. Being outside made her feel better. Cocktail parties were not exactly her scene, and certainly not this kind. The people in the room represented a lot of power and wealth and the very air was charged with it. It was a bit intimidating, especially when you were more used to communing with spiders and squirrels than with people. She was afraid she'd say the wrong thing to the wrong person. One of her flaws was that her mouth sometimes got away from her. She'd say things before thinking about them. This was not always appreciated, and when she was wrong it was mortifying.

Footsteps came down the path and she recognised Chase Montana. She felt her body tense for no reason that made any sense except that he had a magnetism she reacted to involuntarily. She didn't like it. She didn't want to react to this man.

'Nice night,' he said, taking a sip from his drink.

'Yes,' she said. He was awfully tall. Of course, almost anybody was tall next to her five feet two.

'Did you see the mock-up?' he asked.

'Yes.'

'What did you think?' He looked at her with interest, as if it mattered what she thought. It mattered nothing. She was not a potential investor in the project and had no connections with it one way or another. Was he just making conversation?

Not for a minute, came the automatic answer. He was not a man who wasted time making idle chit-chat. He was talking to her for a reason, whatever it was, and what he wanted to know was what she thought of the project.

She hesitated. Watch your mouth, she admonished herself. He glanced down at her and smiled faintly.

'Go ahead.'

'It's going to be a beautiful hotel, and I'm sure the grounds are going to be magnificent.' This was true enough.

'But?'

'I didn't say but.'

His eyes studied her face. 'Ah, but there is a but,' he said slowly. 'I can see it in your eyes. You do not altogether approve.'

No, not altogether. She scrambled for appropriately polite words.

'I don't know all the details and circumstances and I've never been to Ecuador. I don't like giving uninformed opinions.' Boy, that sounded good. She was proud of herself.

His mouth quirked. 'Very commendable. However, you do have an opinion?'

'Of course I have an opinion.' For some reason, his questions made her uneasy. She sipped her drink and looked off into the shadowed gardens. She was truly making an effort to keep control over her tongue but he was not making it easy.

He looked at her questioningly. 'Are you going to tell me?'

The man was impossible. She sighed. 'To tell you the truth, Mr Montana, it bothers me. The hotel is very large. It will hold a lot of people.'

'The better to make money.'

Irritation flared up inside her. Money. As if that excused everything.

'Yes. But that's not what bothers me.'

'The making money part?'

'No. There's nothing wrong with making money. What matters is how, and at what cost, and to whom.'

His eyes narrowed and he studied her for a moment. 'And you have your doubts as to whether this project will be making money in a responsible manner,' he stated slowly.

She looked straight into his eyes and threw caution to the winds. 'Yes. From the information I got from the display, I understand that the hotel will be put in quite an isolated area of primal rainforest. From the photos and that anthropological little blurb on the wall it is obvious that the indigenous people there live very traditional lives and have had little contact with the outside world. Bringing in large numbers of wealthy westerners into a place like that is irresponsible.' So there, she'd said it. He'd asked for it.

His face was shadowed in the dim light. 'Rainforests are big tourist attractions these days,' he commented.

His attitude aggravated her no end. 'I understand that,' she said tightly, 'but a hotel full of people with cameras and video recorders and watches and sunglasses is going to have a big impact on the place and not all positive!' She took a deep breath. 'Everywhere in the world we can see the damage tourists do!' She was off and going. 'In Kenya the wildlife is suffering because too many tourists disturb their natural living rhythms. Tropical reefs are damaged and fish species become extinct because there are too many divers! We're wiping out traditional cultures, sometimes entire tribes by introducing them to the joys and comforts of modern civilisation!'

She stopped herself and drew in a deep breath and stared into the shadowed garden. Protection of the environment was a subject close to her heart, but she did not want to sound like a ranting zealot.

'You cannot hold back progress,' he said mildly.

What a lousy excuse, she wanted to say, but swallowed the words. 'There's progress and progress,' she said stubbornly, trying to keep her cool. 'There's doing it responsibly and doing it irresponsibly. And going by what I've seen and heard about your project I can only conclude that it's not responsible.' This was an understatement, of course. She thought it was a disgrace. She looked at his shadowed face, unwavering. 'And I'm sure I'm not the only one who has voiced these sentiments.'

He inclined his head slightly, his face inscrutable. 'No, indeed, you are not.' He gestured at the house. 'However, none of the people who has done so is present here, so I suggest you keep your opinion to yourself.'

The gall of the man! 'I would have kept it to myself had you not pushed me! You very specifically asked for my opinion and I gave it!'

His mouth curved crookedly. 'Indeed you did. And I compliment you on your very diplomatic language. I have heard the same opinion expressed in much less flattering words.' He took a sip from his drink, his eyes on her face. 'I'd better go inside and tend to my other guests. Enjoy the scenery.'

She watched him stride into the house. Had she made him angry? She couldn't tell and she didn't care. He'd asked for her opinion and she'd given it.

'Enjoy the scenery', he had said. Well, she would. She was in no mood to converse with people who destroyed nature for the sole purpose of adding on to their wealth. She took a deep breath of the fragrant air and glanced around. Massive old trees—oaks and hickories and hemlocks—shaded the house. Delicate Japanese maples with their wine-red foliage added elegance and large azaleas brightened the grounds with splashes of bright colour.

She was not meant to have peace and quiet, because Sean appeared minutes after Chase had gone back into the house. He draped an arm possessively around her and she stiffened instinctively. She had never done that before and she knew it was a sign, clear and immutable in its meaning. It was over between them. She did not love him. She *could* not love him. Her throat ached and she swallowed painfully.

'I was looking for you,' he said, dropping a kiss on her cheek. 'Nice party. What are you doing out here?'

'I just wanted a little fresh air.' Obviously his anger towards her had cooled, but she could not ignore the significance of the incident in the car. She couldn't stay blind to Sean's selfish and disrespectful attitude towards her.

'What do you think of Chase?' he asked.

'Very imposing. Consummately self-confident.'

Sean laughed. 'Too bad his brother Breck isn't here. He's in the Far East negotiating another deal. The two of them make quite a combo. I think I'm going to make out like a bandit on this one,' he said with smug satisfaction. 'Everybody and his dog wants to see the rainforest these days.'

Sean was one of the potential investors of the project, be it a small one, but his enthusiasm was large. He hadn't told her many details and she hadn't understood the extent of the project until she'd seen the mock-up and other displays this evening. She didn't feel like talking to him about it and getting into another argument. One argument with him in a day was quite enough. She said nothing.

His hand stroked the nape of her neck. 'I'm sorry I upset you earlier,' he went on. 'But please be reasonable about this trip.'

Fresh anger rose to her head. She moved away from him, gritting her teeth. Sean's definition of reasonable was giving in to his wishes.

'You don't *have* to go, do you?' he asked when she did not reply.

Despair mixed itself with her anger—a bitter concoction. He had not changed his mind. He didn't take her seriously. She swallowed hard. 'The answer is yes and no. Yes, of course I *have* to go. This is a fantastic opportunity. And no, I don't *have* to go—not as in being obliged to because I'm being ordered by a superior.'

'So it comes down to the fact that you *want* to go.'

Anger was taking the upper hand now. 'Of course I want to go! It'll be good for my career. You don't get it, do you? Tell me honestly why you don't want me to go on this trip!'

'It's dangerous, camping out in the wilds like that. You might catch something.' He was looking the other way as he said it, as if he didn't quite dare to look her in the face.

She gave a mocking little laugh. 'Oh, for heaven's sake! Don't make me laugh.' He was making excuses, as if his objection stemmed from his concern for her welfare rather than his own self-interest.

'You'll be gone a long time.' He looked grim.

'A month. Surely you can survive a month without me.'

'We'll have to cancel next weekend.'

'Yes. I am sorry about that.' They'd been invited by one of his friends to spend a weekend on his luxury yacht cruising the Chesapeake Bay. She'd looked forward to it, but sacrifices had to be made sometimes. Was it too much to ask from a man that on occasion he accommodate a woman's career needs?

Sean sighed impatiently. 'Sky, I needed the time off! I've worked at neck-breaking speed lately and I need some relaxation!'

'You can go without me, Sean.' She felt a wave of fatigue wash over her. She didn't want to have this conversation. It was hopeless and useless, and he simply refused to understand.

His jaw went rigid. His grey eyes looked icy. 'That wasn't the plan. I want you with me.'

'I know, but sometimes plans need to be changed,' she said wearily. He was acting like a spoiled brat. Not an endearing quality in a man— or anyone else, for that matter.

'I thought you'd want to be with me. I thought we . . . had something.'

You're wrong, she thought, feeling sadness overwhelm her. 'I think you're being extremely selfish, Sean. Why can't you see that this trip is important for my career?'

He said nothing. It was a very eloquent silence and she felt her heart sink.

'You don't really think my career is important, do you?' She heard the dull resignation in her own voice. She'd recognised the truth, but had resisted putting it into words until now. 'You seem to think it's some sort of *hobby*.'

'Very few photographers ever make it big, Sky. You know that.'

She tensed. 'I'll make it, Sean. I *am* making it. I've done very well this past year.' Her *Hope* series had been exhibited in the Benedict gallery in Washington D.C. She'd had several very good assignments. It just took time and perseverence in this business. And a lot of hard work. 'I support myself, I pay taxes, I have no debts and I own my own house.'

'A barn, Sky,' he said with a dismissive gesture. 'You live in a barn.' He said it as if she slept in the straw with the pigs.

However, she did live in a barn—a remodelled old red barn—and she loved it. It was certainly an eccentric place to live, but it was spacious, comfortable, unique and it suited her needs perfectly. It was, obviously, not up to Sean's sophisticated standards. Well, she'd had enough of Sean and his sophisticated standards.

'You don't respect my work and you belittle my efforts and you don't like where I live,' she said bitterly. 'I have no idea at all why you're interested in me and why you can't live without me for a month.'

'Don't start, Sky,' he warned.

She gave a derisive little laugh and suddenly the weariness was gone and anger gushed from her. 'I'm starting nothing! I'm finishing something! I cannot tolerate that kind of disrespect from you, Mr Managing Director! You may have a big title and a huge income, but you have a very small mind!' She whirled around and marched away, her legs unsteady. What was it that gave him the right to feel so damned superior? She stormed inside the large party-room, and out of the first door that came into view, straight into a hard, broad chest.

The impact stopped her in her tracks. Her face was pressed against the smooth cotton fabric of a shirt. Her gasp drew in a clean, male scent. Her cheek took in the warmth that came through the shirt. Her body flooded with a tingling, intoxicating warmth.

'Well, well,' Chase drawled. 'Are you running out on my party?' He had an arm around her in an effort to steady her.

She struggled out of his embrace, fighting for composure. 'I'd like to,' she said tightly, 'but I'll have to wait for my ride.' It was not going to be a pleasure trip home. Sean's anger would not suddenly disappear.

He lifted a quizzical brow. 'Not enjoying yourself? Something wrong with the food perhaps?'

'No. Something's wrong with men.'

'That's quite a sweeping statement.'

'I'm sweeping mad.'

He laughed. It was a deep, rich sound, and suddenly she found herself cracking a smile, her sense of humour getting the better of her. His eyes gleamed into hers.

'You have a way with words. So what's wrong with men?'

'They're selfish, manipulative, arrogant and into control,' she said loftily. 'Haven't you watched Oprah lately?'

'I can't say that I have, but I don't consider myself too old to learn. How about a drink to calm you down?'

He wanted to calm her down. She smiled nicely. 'Would you say that to one of your male business friends when he was angry?' Her tone was light.

He frowned, thinking. 'Not exactly like that.'

'You'd slap him on the shoulder and say, You need a drink, man; let's go.'

'I'm afraid if I slapped you on the shoulder you'd crumple.'

She groaned. It was hopeless, hopeless. She couldn't help being small and blonde. She evoked in people protective feelings, which was nice if you came down with galloping pneumonia and needed nursing, but in normal life it was infuriating.

'I don't crumple. I'm very strong, actually, and yes, I would like a drink. Something more potent than champagne—anything.'

Chase studied her with amused curiosity. 'Coming up.'

Moments later she had a glass of whisky soda in her hand and she took a grateful swallow. She wasn't much of a drinker of strong stuff, but on occasion she liked it.

'I like your dress,' he said as his eyes skimmed over her. 'It's very—er—woodsy.'

It was short and supremely simple in line and would have been discreetly elegant had it not been for the exotic pattern of the silk fabric. Its leafy design of many shades of green contrasted with small splashes of vivid red, yellow and blue, which on closer inspection could be identified as parrots hiding in the greenery.

'Thank you,' she said brightly. She wondered if he meant what he said. 'Not everyone shares your opinion.' Sean had been less than enthusiastic and asked why she couldn't have worn something not quite so flamboyant, like basic black. She was not fond of basic black. It made her feel very depressed and depression was not an uplifting emotion.

'Black would look more elegant and sophisticated,' he'd instructed her.

She'd laughed. 'Sean, I thought you'd have noticed by now that I am *not* the elegant, sophisticated type. I crawl around in the woods and commune with bugs and birds. I feel at home in this dress.' She liked being surrounded by trees and bushes and birds, and she loved parrots. And in view of the rainforest hotel project she'd thought the dress eminently appropriate. She'd bought the dress in a sale. It had originally been very expensive, but apparently women with a lot of money had considered the dress too wild for their taste.

Chase's eyes gleamed. 'The parrots I find especially intriguing.'

'Papuan King Parrots,' she informed him. 'Alisterus chloropterus.'

'Ah, an ornithologist,' he stated.

She shook her head. 'A photographer.' She smiled innocently. 'Every time I hike through the woods, I keep looking for parrots. I never see one.'

His mouth quirked. 'Let me do you a favour,' he said. 'Looking for tropical parrots in a forest in Virginia is a losing proposition.'

She bit her lip, trying not to smile. She was not successful. 'It's not nice to shatter someone's dreams, you know.' Her voice was light, yet the atmosphere between them was anything but casual. Something was in the air—something reflected in his eyes, the tone of his voice.

His green eyes did not leave her face. 'Somehow I don't think that's what I'm doing.'

She sipped her drink, saying nothing, feeling her pulse quicken, feeling a strange apprehension.

'So, what else are you interested in, apart from photographing parrots?' he asked casually.

Why didn't she believe he was as casual as he sounded? As if his question had some hidden purpose?

'I like travelling, but I haven't had many chances, and I like hiking and camping and white-water rafting.'

He cocked an eyebrow. 'Really?'

She nodded. 'Yes, really.' She was used to people's surprise. She didn't look the sporty type. She was too small and too blonde and too feminine, and even her short, sporty hairstyle did nothing to dispel that image.

'And you?' she asked. 'What do you do in your spare time? Play golf? Ride horses?'

He inclined his head. 'Of course.' He tossed back the last of his drink, and then someone claimed his attention and she gratefully slipped away.

She wanted to go home. She'd had enough of smiling politely and making conversation for the sake of making conversation. Of course Sean would want to stay. He loved this sort of thing. Networking, it was called—making contacts. She should be networking herself. After all, you could never know where a new assignment could originate, and there were a lot of influential types prancing around here. But tonight she didn't feel up to it. She wanted to go home and cry and wallow in self-pity.

She clenched her hands involuntarily and swallowed at the lump in her throat. When she was nineteen her life had been perfect and she'd thought it was going to be perfect for the rest of her life. By the time she'd turned twenty her world had crumbled around her.

She'd been so young, so idealistic, so full of dreams. It seemed like another lifetime. Now, sometimes, she felt wise and old and cynical. It was not a nice feeling, and not one she intended to cultivate.

She glanced around the room, finding no Sean. She had a raging headache, which was not so surprising considering the circumstances. She'd been up very late last night doing paperwork and reading up on Mexico. The little bit of sleep she'd caught had been fitful and full of confusing dreams. And now this confrontation with Sean... She rubbed her forehead, feeling physically exhausted and emotionally drained.

Where was he? Impatiently she roamed around, her feet hurting. She wasn't used to wearing high heels, although it did give her an enjoyable sense of being a bit taller, and more elegant. Ten minutes later there still was no sign of him. She was beginning to feel uneasy and her head throbbed painfully. On impulse she slipped out of the front door and went in search of Sean's car, a white Pontiac Fiero. She wished she'd come in her own car, an ancient little sky-blue Jeep, so that she wouldn't have been dependent on Sean to see her home. Not that her little Jeep would have felt at home among the lofty vehicles in the parking area, she thought as she scanned the impressive collection of expensive cars. There was no sign of Sean's Fiero.

It was gone, leaving an open space between a shiny charcoal Mercedes Benz and a metallic blue BMW.

For a moment she stood very still, incredulous.

He had left! He had left without her! The swine!

She didn't know a soul at the party. They were miles out in the countryside in an isolated historic plantation house. She didn't even know where she was exactly. Sean had been driving and she hadn't paid much attention.

She'd been dumped. There was no other word for it. Leaving her stranded was Sean's revenge, no doubt. She should have known. She'd told him he had a small mind, and this was proof. No class, no manners. How could she possibly ever have liked the man? It was frightening to think how blind she had been. How hopeful. How stupid. She swallowed painfully.

Her head throbbed and she rubbed her temples. She went back into the house and headed for the bar. She needed a drink, some juice or water. She needed to get rid of this headache—she was beginning to see stars. She was beginning to feel dizzy.

She needed to figure out a way to get home. Surveying the room, she studied the guests. All the men wore very expensive suits. All the women wore very expensive dresses, none with parrots. Not a single familiar face, not a single person she could impose on to take her home. It was almost an hour's drive away. And forget a taxi. It would take care of her food budget for the month even if she could manage to get one out here in the back of beyond, which was highly unlikely.

She asked for a glass of orange juice with ice and went in search of a quiet place and a chair to sit in. The marbled entrance hall was empty. If she sat here for a while, maybe her head would stop hurting. She noticed a door slightly ajar and glimpsed a desk, a bookcase, a large sofa.

A sofa! She pushed the door open and slipped in, closing the door behind her.

She needed to lie down—just for a little while. She was going to pass out if she didn't. She put the glass down on the massive oak desk, using a discarded envelope from the wastebasket as a coaster. Kicking off her high heels, she lay down, closed her eyes and tried to empty her head of all thought. It was heaven. She heard the muted sounds of talking and laughter from other parts of the house. The quiet in this study was like a balm for her tortured head. In a little while she'd get up and tackle the problem of transportation.

*   *   *

When she awoke it was too late to tackle the problem of transportation. It was three o'clock in the middle of the night and the house was silent as a tomb. She felt panic rise and forced it down. This was not the end of the world. It was merely excruciatingly embarrassing.

She swallowed back a laugh. Oh, God, leave it to her to get into a situation like this. She struggled into a sitting position and stared into the darkness until her eyes adjusted. It wasn't all that dark. A wave of moonlight swam through the window, washing the massive wooden desk in a silver sheen.

Her headache was gone. This was good news.

She needed to go to the bathroom. This was bad news.

There was a bathroom off the entrance hall, she had discovered earlier that evening. Unfortunately, running water made noise. What if the green-eyed tiger heard her? At least, she assumed he was asleep somewhere in this mansion. Oh, God. She could see it now. He'd come in search of her in black silk pyjamas. He'd pounce on her.

Well, she simply had no choice. She tiptoed out of the door, across the oriental rug that graced the marble entrance hall. A large, curving staircase swept up regally to the second floor.

She found the bathroom and prayed he would not hear the running of water after she flushed and washed. The mirror produced a nightmarish sight. Her mascara and eyeliner had smeared all over the place. Her hair was standing out in every direction and looked like a bleached mop in the garish light. It wasn't bleached. It was perfectly honest blonde hair, but somehow she looked like a tramp, especially with her dress now wrinkled disastrously. Poor abused parrots. She bit her lip and chuckled.

She tiptoed back into the study and sat down on the sofa, waiting with bated breath for sounds of footsteps in the house. Nothing. After a few minutes she began to breathe more easily.

She needed to collect her thoughts.

Leaving the house was out of the question. She had no transportation and only a vague idea of the general location of the place. She was at least an hour's drive away from her barn, not a distance she could walk. Calling Beth, her friend, or her mother in the dead of night to come and get her was asking no small favour, but it would do no good because she couldn't give any directions. This left her with only one possibility.

She'd have to make her presence known and ask for help.

Help from Chase Montana, who was asleep somewhere in this sprawling plantation house.

For obvious reasons three o'clock in the morning was not a good time to go in search of him and awaken him. Closing her eyes, she visualised him asleep in a big bed, wearing black silk pyjamas, or maybe nothing. Probably nothing. She imagined touching his arm, trying to stir him from sleep. In her mind she could just see him leap, naked from the bed, growling. She grinned to herself. Well, she could still laugh.

There was no good time for this confrontation, but the morning was better than now. She sighed and smoothed the fabric of her dress. Silk dresses were not meant to be slept in. She groaned. She would look a disaster in the morning.

Her eyes caught a framed photograph on the desk, captured by the moonlight, and she could not resist having a closer look. It was a starchy family portrait: father, mother and two young teenage sons. One of the sons was Chase—a much younger version of the one she'd met last night. The other was obviously his younger brother. The portrait was agonisingly formal. The father wore a pin-striped suit and looked grim. The mother's dress was conservatively elegant and she wore a strand of pearls and a stilted smile. Both boys wore jackets, shirts and dark ties, and their hair had been slicked back. The younger boy's smile was a frozen grimace, much like Chase's. Yet there was a difference in their expressions. Chase's eyes had a devilish gleam in them. She'd seen that same gleam last night. A sudden little shiver ran down her back. She wasn't looking forward to facing him in the morning.

She went back to the sofa, lay down and closed her eyes. She might as well sleep some more. There was nothing else to do. If only she could pick up the phone and talk to Beth. Beth would die laughing, but not at three in the morning. Sky felt a spasm of pain and pushed it away. Beth and Kevin were moving to North Dakota in a couple of months. They'd been part of her life for a long time, ever since college. They were her only two close friends who had known Josh. Their departure would leave a terrible hole in her life.

She awoke to a grey morning and a sense of doom. No sunlight streamed through the uncurtained windows and it did not look like a spring morning. She grimaced. She could have done with a little sunshine to give her courage. It was just after seven, according to her watch.

Coffee. Her body was begging for a cup of strong coffee. Quietly she moved to the door and carefully opened it a crack. Muted noises reached her ear. Somebody was stirring around somewhere on the ground floor.

Chase Montana?

With her heart in her throat, she slipped back into the bathroom and washed her face and hands. She rubbed at the remainders of mascara and eye-liner with a tissue and some hand lotion that was thoughtfully provided. She had a comb in her bag and she pulled it through her hair. There was nothing she could do about the dress. It was a sorry sight. Quickly, noiselessly, she went back into the office and slipped on her shoes. She straightened herself to her full five feet two inches and took a deep, fortifying breath. It was time to face the tiger.

First, of course, she had to find him. She knew where the kitchen was. Platters of food had emerged from it last night. It was the logical place to start the search.

The kitchen door was closed, but it opened before she could reach to do so herself. And there he was, Chase Montana himself, wearing casual cotton trousers and an open-necked shirt, a cup of coffee in his hand.

His dark brows arched in surprise, then settled in their natural place again. His eyes narrowed and his mouth curled in a predatory grin and the silence crackled with tension.

'Well, well,' he drawled. 'Look who's here.'

CHAPTER TWO

Sky's heart sank at the tone of his voice and she felt a nervous wobble in her knees. Since she wasn't given to wobbly knees, this was not promising.

She had decided that the only way to deal with this most embarrassing situation was to come right out and tell it the way it was. His tone of voice, however, was not encouraging and did not help her confidence. The man had a terrible effect on her equilibrium, physically as well as emotionally, and she couldn't help feeling swamped with trepidation.

'I fell asleep in your office,' she said. 'I'm sorry.'

He put his coffee down and thrust his hands in his pockets, surveying her with narrow-eyed suspicion. 'It's an interesting technique,' he said calmly. 'Do you do this sort of thing often?'

' "Technique"?' she echoed, uncomprehending.

He nodded. 'I've been told that meeting available men is difficult these days. Entire books are written on the subject.'

Words failed her. She had seen those books. *How to Catch a Rich Man*, *Loving a Wealthy Man is Easier*. Fury and humiliation washed over her. It took all her strength to calm herself enough to speak.

'I've never found it necessary to resort to those techniques, Mr Montana. And if I did, may I assure you that I wouldn't choose you as my victim. You're not my type.'

29

He was absolutely, positively not her type. He was too arrogant, too smooth, too sure of himself. He ravaged beautiful rainforests.

He quirked a mocking brow. 'Is that right?' he asked slowly.

She straightened her spine and stared hard into his cool green eyes. 'Yes, that's right.' It was difficult to look dignified in a wrinkled jungle dress, and she was well aware of it, but she'd be damned if she'd let him intimidate her.

His gaze skimmed over her from top to toe. 'Then please enlighten me as to why you ended up stowing away here.'

'I didn't stow away! I simply lay down on the sofa in your office. I had an excruciating headache.' And I felt miserable and exhausted, she added silently.

'A headache?' You've got to be joking, his tone said.

'Yes. A real blaster.' She looked at him contemptuously. 'Believe me, seducing you or any other male was the last thing on my mind. All I wanted was to get rid of the pain.' She swung around and marched determinedly to the door. She was leaving. She would walk. She would hitch a ride on a manure truck—anything to get away from this insufferable male who thought she'd hid in his office for some devious purpose.

She was not fast enough.

He caught her by the wrist. 'Where are you going?' he demanded.

'I'm leaving!' His big hand encircled her wrist in a painful grip. 'Let go of my hand!'

'You have a car here?'

'No! I'll walk!'

He released his grip on her. 'I don't think that would be wise.' He looked meaningfully at her wrinkled party dress and her high-heeled shoes. 'It's going to rain and I don't think you're dressed appropriately for a hike in the country at seven o'clock on a Saturday morning.'

She wasn't. Of course she wasn't. She glared into his cool green eyes. 'You owe me an apology,' she said between clenched teeth.

'Not until I know why you are here.'

'I told you!'

'Why do I have trouble believing this headache story?'

'I have no idea!' She had no idea what the matter was with this man. Why he looked at her like this. Why he had this devastating effect on her nerves.

He leaned casually against the door-post and crossed his arms. 'Well, let's go over the facts. Your name is Sky Malone and you're a photographer.'

'Yes,' she said, staring straight into his eyes.

'And supposedly you came here with Sean Kendall.'

'Not supposedly. I did.'

He nodded. 'All right, you did.'

She gave an exasperated sigh. 'Would you please explain to me what this is all about? I don't feel like being interrogated at seven in the morning!'

He nodded agreeably. 'I suppose it would be civil of me to offer you a seat and a cup of coffee. Come along.' He held the kitchen door open for her and waved her in. He offered her a chair. The perfect gentleman, he was. She sat down at the scrubbed wooden table. She didn't have a choice.

It was a big, yet cosy country kitchen and empty of other people. The coffee smelled heavenly. She watched as he poured her a cup. His arm was tanned and muscular with a light sprinkling of dark hair. His hand was big and strong. She felt a tiny twinge of... excitement, apprehension. She drew in a slow breath. It was just a man's arm, a man's hand.

'Sugar? Cream?' he enquired politely.

'Both, please.'

He put the cup in front of her as well as a sugar bowl and a small carton of cream from the refrigerator. He refilled his own mug and sat down opposite her.

'You told me you didn't stay the night because you had designs on my body,' he stated casually. 'So what else could it be?'

'Your silver,' she said promptly. 'Maybe I wanted to steal you blind and escape in the middle of the night.'

'Only we have a burglar alarm system and all hell would have broken loose if you'd tried to leave.'

She shrugged.

He took a swallow of coffee. 'Did you find any silver that looked interesting?' he asked with mock-interest.

'None.' She put three generous spoonfuls of sugar in her cup.

'Well, that's a relief.' He looked pointedly at her stirring her coffee. 'You have a sweet tooth?'

'Not normally, but it appears I need the energy.' She drank greedily, feeling the sweet, rich mixture slide comfortingly into her system.

He leaned back in his chair. 'So it wasn't my body and it wasn't the silver. Interesting.' He drank his coffee and studied her over the rim of his cup as if she were some fascinating but dangerous insect.

She gritted her teeth. 'Are you always so suspicious of people? Do you have some sort of paranoia?'

'Not until recently.' He smiled. It was not a friendly smile and she felt her apprehension grow. She fortified herself with another deep drink of coffee.

'And what happened recently?' she asked, trying to sound casual.

He gave her a penetrating stare. 'Somebody brought a lawsuit against me.'

She took in the hard line of his jaw. 'Oh, really? Are the environmentalists after you?' A smile escaped her at the thought. She couldn't help it.

'You find this amusing?' he asked coolly.

Her smile widened. 'Actually, yes, I do,' she said recklessly. 'That hotel in Ecuador is a terrible idea.'

'So you told me yesterday.'

'And that makes me a criminal?'

'No, that does not make you a criminal.' He came to his feet, picked up the coffee-pot and refilled both their cups.

She added four spoons of sugar while he watched. He made her uncomfortable. The uneasiness crawled through her blood. Maybe he thought she was here to find out more about him as a person, to infiltrate the lair of the money-hungry tiger and dig up some dirt. Character assassination was a popular technique in court cases. She looked up from her cup and met his eyes.

'If you're accusing me of something, I have the right to know.' She clenched her hands. 'All I did was fall asleep on your sofa and now you interrogate me as if I were a common criminal! I don't know anything about that lawsuit and I am not here to dig up dirt on you, if that's what you're thinking!'

He eyed her narrowly. 'Unfortunately, I don't feel reassured.'

'You think I'm lying?'

He shrugged. 'I don't know you, do I? I find it very suspicious to find you here in this house. I'm simply trying to ascertain what the reason might be.' He paused fractionally. 'Apart from that headache story.'

She covered her face with her hands and moaned. There was no way she was going to convince him of her innocence.

'What happened to Sean last night?' he continued. 'You said you came with him to the party.'

'Yes, I did.' She lowered her hands and clasped them together on the table in front of her.

'But you didn't leave with him.'

'No, I did not.' In the circumstances, maybe that was suspicious. He didn't like Sean; she was quite sure of that.

'Why not?'

Well, what could she say? The truth and nothing but the truth: He dumped me.

'He left without me,' she said, which sounded a bit more dignified. She tried not to look at the small wisp of dark chest hair that peeked out from his open-necked shirt. Everything about him seemed to disturb her—his eyes, his voice, his damned chest hair.

His brows arched. 'That would indicate a certain lack of manners, wouldn't you say?'

'Absolutely.' She could only agree. 'I think he was having a tantrum.' She swallowed a nervous chuckle. The situation was beginning to take on farcical overtones.

'A tantrum? I thought children had tantrums.'

'Some men have them too,' she said lightly. 'When women don't fall all over themselves pleasing them.'

'I see. So he was having a tantrum because you were not falling all over yourself pleasing him.'

She nodded, trying not to smile. 'You could say that, yes. I'm going to Mexico for a month and we had an argument about it in your lovely garden.'

'Ah, after which you threw yourself into my arms. You fit quite nicely actually; did you notice?'

She gave him a withering look, and his mouth twitched.

'Just a casual observation. When I hold a woman close in my arms I can't help noticing the feel and shape of her.'

Her heart began to race at the image and she remembered very well the feel of his hard chest against her cheek and the warm male smell of him. Oh, God, this was insanity. 'I hope it was a big thrill for you,' she said caustically.

'It was.' His smile showed even white teeth. 'Now tell me, what's the problem with your going to Mexico?'

The question was posed casually. They were having a casual conversation, were they? She didn't believe it for a minute.

'As far as I am concerned it's not a problem at all. I consider it a wonderful professional opportunity.'

He nodded. 'But Sean found it a problem,' he surmised.

'Yes, he did, and it's none of your business.' He was beginning to annoy her severely. She didn't like that gleam in his eyes—an odd mixture of amusement and suspicion. She couldn't figure out what he was thinking and feeling about her and it threw her off-balance.

He gave her an assessing look. 'Sean felt he couldn't live without you for that long. He could not imagine that you would choose to go on a trip to Mexico over being with him.'

She felt a rush of anger. 'Oh, so he told you, did he?'

He gave a half-smile. 'No. I've known Sean for a while and it's simply an educated guess. Why are you going to Mexico?'

'A friend of mine is leading a small research team and I've been asked to come along as the photographer. There's not much money in it, but the experience is worth a lot and it'll be a new environment for me, and that's always very inspiring.' She bit her lip, feeling a pang of bitter pain. 'Unfortunately, Sean does not think my work is very important. He said as much yesterday.' Her voice wobbled suddenly and it made her angry.

'And you do not take that kindly.'

'No,' she said tightly. 'I told him I wasn't going to tolerate his disrespect and . . .' She hesitated and stopped.

'And what?' he prompted.

Suddenly it was hard not to smile. 'I told him he had a big title and a big salary and a small mind. He didn't like that. I think leaving without me was his idea of revenge.'

'How very childish of him.' Chase smiled a lazy smile. 'So, here you are, stranded,' he concluded. He seemed to find the idea amusing.

She finished her coffee and pushed the cup away from her. 'If you wouldn't mind telling me directions to this place, I'll ask my mother to come and get me. I wasn't paying attention where we were going yesterday.'

'You live with your mother?'

'No. I have my own place, but my parents don't live far.'

He leaned back in his chair. 'And what is your mother going to think when she arrives here and sees you like this?'

Sky shrugged. 'I'll tell her what happened and she'll think it's hilarious. She has quite a sense of humour. Besides, my mother doesn't worry about my morals.'

'She doesn't? Why is that?'

She sighed. 'Because there's nothing to worry about.'

He nodded. 'I'm glad to hear that,' he said piously and she wanted to throw her coffee at him. She managed to control herself.

'None the less,' he went on, 'let's not inconvenience your mother this morning. I'll drive you home.'

'That's not necessary. I live almost an hour's drive from here.'

'No problem. First we'll have breakfast.'

She stiffened. She didn't want him to drive her home, but it didn't seem as if she had much choice. It was clear that he was a man who did what he wanted to do and arguing was going to get her nowhere.

'I don't want any breakfast, thank you. I'd just as soon get going so I can get out of these clothes and into the shower. I feel stupid sitting here in this ridiculous dress.'

'You can get out of the dress and into a shower here.' He held up his hand as if to ward off a refusal. 'Please be my guest, since you are already, anyway.'

'I don't have any clothes to change into. I didn't come prepared for this...excursion, even if you do think so.'

'I'm sure we can find you something. Come along. You take that shower while I cook us some breakfast.'

'Why don't you just take me home?'

He shrugged lightly. 'I'm in no hurry.' And I call the shots, his eyes said. Without me you're going nowhere.

She was at his mercy.

'I hope you're enjoying this little power game,' she said with cold disdain.

One dark brow lifted sardonically. 'Power game? Let's not be melodramatic, shall we? I simply prefer to have some breakfast before starting my day, and I'm offering you the same, as well as a shower and a change of clothes. I'm only trying to be a good host.' He smiled politely and gestured at the open kitchen door. 'Come with me.'

She followed him up the curving staircase, feeling frustrated and out of control. She didn't like feeling out of control. The man's attitude displayed a confusing mixture of charm, suspicion and politeness and it was difficult to deal with.

He threw open the door to a large bedroom. 'The bathroom is through there,' he said, pointing across the room. 'Help yourself to whatever you need.' He opened a wardrobe. 'There are clothes in here.' He gave her a quick, assessing look. 'I'm sure you'll find something that will fit.'

She glanced at the clothes. Expensive, fashionable clothes. 'Whose are these? Your wife's?'

He gave a half-smile. 'No. If I had a wife, believe me she would not have her own room or her own bed. She'd share mine.'

'She'd have to want to,' she blurted out. Oh, God, why couldn't she control her tongue?

His green eyes met hers. 'Oh,' he said slowly, meaningfully, 'she'd want to.'

Against her will she had to admit that this was probably true. Disturbing images flooded her mind and she pushed them away with an effort. 'Sure of yourself, aren't you?' she asked, putting a good dose of mockery in her voice.

He smiled. 'Oh, very.' He glanced around the room. 'This is my—er—sister's room.'

His—er—sister's room. Sure it was. She gave him a sceptical look and his green eyes gleamed. He moved back to the door. 'I'll start breakfast. Do you have any particular dislikes or allergies?'

Yes, you, she wanted to say, but didn't.

'No. I like everything.'

'A woman after my own heart,' he said, and for
the second time in minutes she was tempted to throw
something at him. He closed the door and was gone.

'All men are scum', a fifteen-year-old cousin had
told her not long ago, trying to sound important
and world-wise. Well, Sky was beginning to think
the kid was right. All men except Josh, she amended
automatically as she glowered at the closed bedroom
door. But Josh was dead. Josh had not been scum.
Josh had been wonderful. They'd shared a marriage licence, a tiny apartment, a cosy bed, very
little money and a wealth of dreams.

It would never be like that again. She was no
longer the starry-eyed teenage bride. There would
never be another Josh. She did not expect there to
be, of course. She was older now, she had a career,
and her life had moved on. The men she met were
older and established in a career.

She glanced around. The bedroom that belonged
to the—er—sister was beautiful. It was the sort of
room you saw in expensive, glossy magazines. A
huge canopy bed commanded the room, the bed-
linen lacy and white. The furniture in the room was
all antique and gleamed with good care and lots of
polishing.

The bathroom was sumptuous with a gorgeous,
claw-foot bath and shiny white tiles. An enormous,
luxuriant fern cascaded down from a hanging pot.
It looked so perfect, she had to touch it to see that
it was real and not silk. It was real. Open shelving
revealed stacks of fluffy cotton towels in pale jade-
green, soft rose and white. Bathroom toiletries
abounded—expensive   soaps,   bubble   bath,
shampoos, talcum powder and body lotions.

Having a bath here would be no punishment; she might as well get to it.

As she sat in the steaming, fragrant water, she contemplated men, more specifically the men she had known since she had become a widow at nineteen. It was not encouraging. None of them had taken her career as a nature and wildlife photographer very seriously. It was a nice hobby and certainly it was nice that she earned a little money with it, but their own careers were so much more important and serious and so much more lucrative. The more money you made, the more prestige and status you had.

Well, she liked money well enough and earning more would not hurt her feelings, but she resented having her career being judged by some monetary value standard.

She'd known an architect, a business consultant and now Sean, who was the managing director of a computer-systems design firm. All of them had been nice and charming and had taken her out to lovely dinners and given her roses and wanted to sleep with her. All of them had thought she was beautiful and amusing and enjoyed her company. All of them had thought she took pretty pictures and why didn't she move out of that rustic barn and into a decent town house somewhere closer to the civilised world like Washington or Richmond? Surely she could take pictures there? It would be so much more convenient.

Why did she always end up with the wrong men? It was a curse. She stared morosely at the bubbles. She was not going to find another man who was right for her. She should just give it up, stop hoping

for the impossible. As a single woman she could
live a rewarding life; the magazines said so.
Marriage was not the only road to happiness.
Sometimes it was the road to hell. She should keep
that in mind, always.

She'd forget about men and focus all her energies
on her career. Eventually she would be recognised
for her exceptional work—her creative visions, her
artistic interpretations. She would get big assignments and travel all around the world. She'd have
exhibits in prestigious galleries. Her first exhibit was
already behind her and had been very successful.
Surely others would follow. This last year had been
very promising.

She didn't need a man in her life.

It sounded so brave, so in control.

But why didn't she feel brave? Why did she feel
alone and scared? Why was she sitting here in this
warm, bubbly bath with the tears running down
her face?

Half an hour later she emerged from the bathroom,
fragrant and clean and back in control of her
wayward emotions. She wrapped a dry towel
around herself and went back into the bedroom in
search of something to wear.

Inspecting the clothes a little more carefully, she
tried to imagine the woman who owned them. There
were clothes for every possible occasion, from
evening gowns to jeans and leggings, all of them
with very impressive labels—if that sort of thing
impressed you. The owner of the clothes was young,
no doubt beautiful and had great taste—classy but

with an obvious touch of whimsy. She was also, miracles of miracles, small like Sky herself.

Sky selected a pair of white leggings and an over-sized black T-shirt that hung halfway down her thighs. It obliterated most of her shape and the colour black seemed appropriate for the occasion. She slipped on a pair of black canvas trainers and glanced in the mirror. She looked casual enough for an overcast Saturday morning in May, and she had no desire to wear somebody else's expensive silk shirt and designer jeans. She'd probably spill something on them and ruin them and then feel obliged to replace them, which would cost her a fortune she didn't have.

Wonderful smells wafted forth as she opened the kitchen door—bacon, toast. She was ravenous.

Chase was standing at the stove and turned as he heard her come in. His gaze skimmed over her in amused surprise.

'Black?' he enquired. 'After that exuberant parrot dress, you put on something black?'

'I'm in mourning,' she said and sat down.

His mouth quirked. 'And for whom or what are you in mourning?'

'The death of an illusion,' she said theatrically. 'I'm giving up men.'

One corner of his mouth turned up. 'You do have a sense of the dramatic.' He poured her a glass of orange juice. 'Sean really got to you, didn't he?'

'It wasn't just him. There were others just like him. I have a fifteen-year-old cousin who says all men are scum.' She sighed heavily. 'I've come to the sad conclusion she's right.'

'I can see it breaks your heart,' he said, deadpan.

He had no idea what was in her heart, and she was going to leave it that way if she could help it. She took a drink from her orange juice. 'Actually, come to think of it, it's a great relief to finally come to that conclusion.' She smiled breezily. 'Now I can just put it all behind me and go on. No more men. Period. Tomorrow I will wear red and rejoice my freedom.'

He shook his head slowly. 'Such a barren life. Such long, lonely nights. No hugs and kisses.' He looked into her eyes and her heart went wild. There was something undefinable in those eyes that made her feel suddenly light-headed. She struggled for composure and shrugged lightly.

'There's more to life than sex,' she said loftily.

He gave her a look of mock-surprise. 'Really? What?'

Dreams, she thought silently.

She groaned. 'Can we please change the subject?'

'I'm quite enjoying myself.'

'Well, I'm not. I think you ought to tell me about that lawsuit.'

Silence. There was an instant change of atmosphere. The air turned chilly. His eyes narrowed, the smile vanished. 'I'd rather not. It would ruin my appetite.' His mouth twisted in distaste.

She tensed. 'I have a right to know what you're accusing me of.'

'I haven't accused you of anything.'

'All right, you're suspecting me of something!'

He shrugged. 'Forget it.'

She didn't want to forget it, and he wasn't going to forget it either, she was sure, but she doubted she was going to get anything out of him. All she had to do was look at the tough line of his jaw and the inscrutable expression on his face and know that he wasn't going to do a thing he didn't want to do. She twisted the juice glass between her hands. One moment he was warm and smiling, the next he was cold and inscrutable. It was a dangerous combination.

She sipped her juice, deciding she'd better not push the subject. 'Tell me about your business,' she suggested. 'How many hotels does your company own?'

He took some eggs out of the refrigerator. 'I'd rather have you tell me about your business. Do you work for a company or organisation?'

His reaction surprised her a little. Given a choice, most people preferred talking over listening. 'I work freelance,' she answered. 'I take assignments as they come. For magazines and organisations, whatever, and I'm represented by a stock company which sells my photos to magazines, calendar companies, audio-visual firms, and whoever needs pictures.'

'Do you like your work?'

'Oh, yes. I wouldn't want to do anything else.' She glanced out of the window. It was still grey and cheerless outside and the sun was having no luck whatsoever. Clouds hung low in the sky and the general gloom seemed to fit her mood.

A few minutes later breakfast was ready and Chase sat down across from her. The eggs were done just right, as was the bacon and toast. There was a jar of orange-blossom honey and one of blackberry preserve.

'I'd expected a flock of servants in this place,' she commented as she buttered the hot toast.

'They're on vacation, except Mrs Lumpkins, and she'll be in later.'

The phone rang. 'Excuse me,' he said and reached for the receiver hanging on the wall and gave his name. 'Hello, Michelle? Is that you?'

Michelle. A woman's name. Sky watched him as he talked.

'I didn't hear you.' A pause. 'No, I was not asleep. I've just finished breakfast. How's Rome?'

He listened, his face faintly amused. 'Good. Why don't you give me the details?' He began to scribble on a pad as he listened. He began to smile.

'Michelle, you've made a coup! Excellent work! Now, when are you coming home?'

He nodded and wrote something down. 'Of course I will pick you up. Just tell me how many suitcases full of clothes you've bought. Do I need the van? Or will the Maserati do?'

He grinned at whatever the woman was saying. 'See you soon,' he said and replaced the receiver.

'Your—er—sister, I suppose?' Sky asked. She couldn't help herself.

Something glinted in his eyes. 'Yes. She has a great head for business and she helped me out with a job in Rome.'

'It must be nice to have such a brilliant sister,' she said sweetly.

'I'm a lucky man. More juice?'

'No, thank you. I'd like to go now. All I have is my parrot dress since I didn't find any interesting silver, so the Maserati will do.' She smiled winningly into his eyes. The situation tickled her sense of the absurd.

His green eyes glinted. 'The Maserati it will be.'

Not much later they drove down the long, shaded drive to the narrow road that meandered lazily through the hilly countryside. A rabbit hopped across the road, narrowly missing a messy death.

They made casual conversation, or at least it seemed casual. She couldn't escape the uneasy suspicion that his questions all had a purpose. Half an hour later the first big raindrops hit the windscreen and soon after that they were driving through a veritable deluge. Beyond the car windows there was nothing but a sea of grey. The wipers wiped frantically, unable to keep up with the onslaught.

'I hope you know this road well,' she said, speaking loudly to be heard above the sound of the water pounding on the car roof. Driving in a downpour like this was not one of her favourite pastimes.

'Blindly,' he answered, irony in his voice.

He was a competent driver, she could tell. Nerves of steel. Just the same, she decided to keep quiet and not distract his attention from his driving. She studied his face. His profile was strong and angular, like an interesting wood carving, his nose curved, his jaw square and jutting out rather imperiously. His shoulders were broad and his back was straight, his posture one of easy confidence. The hands on the steering-wheel were tanned and strong. He radiated dynamism, self-assurance and an undeniable virility. Unfortunately she was very much aware of it and very much not immune to it. There was an unmistakable magnetism about him that was hard to fight.

An agonised splintering sound penetrated the monotonous sound of pounding rain, followed by

the dull thud of something crashing to the ground
somewhere near by. Chase cursed under his breath,
pulled the car to the side of the road and came to
a stop. Narrow-eyed, he peered through the grey
wall of rain.

'I think something's blocking the road.' He
turned on the emergency lights and opened the
door. The next moment he disappeared into the
torrent of rain. He was back moments later,
drenched to the skin, hair plastered to his head.

'It's a dead tree limb. I'm going to move it; just
stay put.'

'I'll help,' she said and reached for the door-
handle.

'No!' he bellowed. 'I can handle it! Stay in the
car!'

'You've got to be kidding,' she murmured to
herself as she leaped out of the car. The rain beat
into her face, cold and stinging. Within seconds her
clothes were drenched. She followed Chase a few
yards down the road where a tree limb lay diag-
onally across the narrow road, blocking both lanes.
It was not huge, but it was long. Had Chase not
stopped so quickly, they might have run right into
it. If he'd gone only a little faster, it might have
come crashing down on to the car.

'What is the matter with you?' he shouted. 'I
said I can handle it!'

'I love rain,' she shouted back. 'And two of us
can do this better than one.' She examined the position of the branch. 'I think we should——'

'I'm going to move it from this end,' he inter-
rupted and shot out a set of instructions at her,
which she followed without comment, at least until

she lost her foothold in the mud by the side of the road and fell sideways into the muck. Muttering curses, she came back to her feet.

It took a while, but eventually they managed to move the tree limb off the road. In the process they'd made themselves look like a couple of filthy drowned rodents. Although he had managed to stay solidly on both feet, Chase didn't look much better than she, Sky noticed with satisfaction.

They raced back to the car and crawled in, dragging in water and mud and leaves and twigs. The immaculate Maserati would never be the same again. They looked at each other while catching their breath.

Laughter bubbled up inside her. It was difficult to imagine that the imposing business tycoon in the impeccable suit she had met yesterday was the same person as the mud-streaked, rain-soaked man facing her now.

He smiled, looking into her eyes. 'You do amaze me, Sky Malone,' he said slowly. She couldn't take her eyes away from him, from the look on his face. She felt oddly breathless and it had nothing to do with lugging the tree limb off the road.

'Why?' she asked lightly, determined that he shouldn't see the effect he had on her. 'Because I got out in the rain and helped you?'

'You don't look like the type.'

Of course she didn't. She looked like the delicate type who wouldn't want to ruin her hair. She wiped the dripping strands out of her face. 'Well, I am the type.'

His eyes did not leave her face. She felt warm under his regard. There was something in his eyes—

something dangerous and exciting—and she shivered suddenly.

'Sky. . .' His voice caressed her name. 'I've never heard that name. Is there a story behind it?'

'Not really a story. My parents are nature lovers and they wanted something natural, but they thought Daisy and Rose were a little worn. So they came up with Sky. My brother's called Rock, but everybody calls him Rocky.'

Rock, unfortunately, was not a very appropriate name for her wandering brother. Rocky was not a rock. He was more like a wave, or a breeze, always on the move, going somewhere, doing something, mostly on, under, or in the water—sailing, scuba-diving, kayaking down wild rivers.

'Rocky?' Chase's face froze and again there was that cold, ruthless look on his face and all the lightness was gone. 'I see,' he said slowly, wariness in his eyes. The atmosphere changed suddenly. A feeling of dread chilled her blood.

She wondered what he saw. She didn't like the probing look in his eyes, as if he tried to look straight through her. She frowned.

'What's wrong with the name Rocky?'

'Nothing, nothing. It just reminded me of something.' He turned on the ignition, revved the motor too fast and shuddered back on to the road.

'Is something wrong?' she asked.

He stared straight ahead of him. 'I'm filthy, wet and frozen. How far are we from your place?' His voice was coolly impatient.

'About ten miles.'

They drove in silence. It was not a good silence. Something had happened and she had no idea what.

It was still raining, but the worst of it was over by the time they reached the gravel road to her house.

She pointed. 'It's over there.'

'I see a red barn,' he said.

'That's it. I live in a barn.'

He stopped in front of the house, not turning off the engine.

'You'd better come in to clean off,' she suggested. 'I can return you the favour of a shower, but clean clothes will be a problem.' She frowned. 'I can put your things through the washer and drier, but it will take a while.' An hour, at least. Oh, please don't let him accept, she prayed.

'Not necessary. If I can just wash my face and hands, I'll be fine.'

'Yes, of course. I can give you a bath-towel to put around your shoulders to keep you warm.' She opened the door and got out. They walked around to the back door, which was closer to the bathroom, and took off their shoes. He followed her into the kitchen and glanced around. She watched his face, trying to guess what he thought as he surveyed the place she called home.

For a barn, it was small. For a house it was big, even more so because there were no interior walls except around the bathroom. A breakfast-bar was all that separated the kitchen from the large living area furnished with an eclectic mixture of comfortable furniture—deep sofas, an enormous round coffee-table, big floor cushions. Large-leafed plants brought greenery into the house. A massive, cast-iron wood stove dominated one wall. It kept her comfortably warm all winter.

There was no ceiling, and, looking up, there was a view, high up, of rough, unpainted roof beams. Halfway up and about a fourth across, a hayloft now served as a sleeping-loft, which could be reached by a simple open-stepped wooden staircase. The loft was surrounded by a wooden rail, over which hung a bright Indian rug.

'Interesting,' he said, looking back at her. 'Did you remodel this place?'

'My brother and some friends helped me, but I designed it this way. I like open spaces. I don't like small rooms and walls and doors.'

'Your brother must be very handy.'

Sky smiled. 'Oh, he is! He can do anything with his hands and I couldn't have done this without him. It was quite overwhelming at first. A painter had used it as a studio. It had been weatherised, and the basic plumbing was there, but it wasn't really a place to live in on a permanent basis.' She wiped the wet hair out of her face. 'Well, the bathroom is over there. Take any of the towels. I'll make you a cup of coffee.'

He moved towards the bathroom door. 'Don't bother.'

He was back minutes later, his face and hands clean, a big blue towel slung over his shoulder. 'I'll return it.'

She nodded. 'Are you sure you don't want a cup of coffee?'

'I'm fine.' He opened the door.

'Thank you for driving me home,' she said, not knowing what else to say. His eyes met hers, but there was nothing there, nothing but green inscrutability.

He inclined his head. 'It was...interesting meeting you.' He walked out and closed the door behind him. Glancing out of the window, she watched him stride across the brick terrace and out of sight around the side of the barn where the Maserati was parked.

She expelled a sigh of relief, feeling tension drain from her. She hadn't realised how tense she had been; it was disturbing. Chase Montana was potent stuff, and she was happy to be rid of him.

Now for a long hot shower.

Ten minutes later, having washed and shampooed away all traces of mud and muck, she skipped quickly up the stairs to the sleeping-loft to get dressed. Jeans and a sweatshirt would do. A red sweatshirt. She grinned to herself as she pulled it on over her head. Rejoicing was so much more positive than mourning. Being cheerful felt so much better than being dispirited.

Having dressed, she made a pot of coffee and skipped out of the door to the mailbox. It had stopped raining, but everything was wet and green and the trees were dripping.

She riffled through the stack of what looked like mostly junk mail, then saw the brightly coloured postcard, featuring an idyllic tropical island scene and the information that Fiji was paradise. A card from Rocky. She grinned as she deciphered his hastily written words.

Hey. Blue Sky!

Hope all is well with you. I'm doing fine. Sailing to the Philippines with an eccentric French poet and his neurotic wife, a Canadian ortho-

paedic surgeon and an ancient German opera
singer—female. I'm learning a lot. Hugs, Rocky.

Sky laughed. 'Oh, Rocky,' she said out loud,
'you're nuts.'

The towel Chase had borrowed was returned by mail
in a large padded envelope. Inside Sky found a card
with the Montana Group logo. 'Thanks', it read in
a large scrawl. It was all it said and Chase had
signed it himself. She stared at the signature and
shivered. She didn't know why. She couldn't get
away from a terrible sense of foreboding every time
she thought of him, which, unfortunately, she had
done much too much in the last two days.

Now that she had an address, she returned the
clothes she had borrowed the same way. She felt a
sudden twinge of mischief as she wondered what
Chase's secretary would think as she opened the
envelope addressed to him and found women's
clothes inside.

Sky was cataloguing images the next evening
when the doorbell rang. She opened the door. Chase
Montana loomed over her and her heart made a
wild leap, then began to race with sudden dread.

Chase did not look happy. His green eyes were
cold and his face was grim. He wore a suit and tie
and had apparently come straight from his office.
He had a folded newspaper in his hand.

Sky took a fortifying breath. 'Hi,' she said
bravely, determined to keep her cool.

'I want a word with you.' It sounded more like
a command than a request.

'Of course; come in.' She closed the door behind him. 'Have a seat.'

'I'll stand.'

She clenched her teeth. Damn the man!

He looked aside suddenly, his gaze caught by the photo collage on the wall. It was a large display of an ever-changing selection of her pictures. It gave her a chance to study and analyse them any time she looked at them. The wall worked like a magnet to visitors, who couldn't resist looking at the images portrayed there, and obviously Chase was no different. His eyes were riveted to the photos, his expression one of total concentration.

She watched him, fascinated by the intent look on his face, the sharp eyes, wondering what he thought.

With what seemed like an effort he pulled himself away and fastened his penetrating gaze on her. For a moment he stared at her in silence, then with a sudden forceful gesture he flung the newspaper on to the coffee-table.

Automatically she glanced at the paper. *Washington Post*, business section. A piece of writing was circled with a thick red felt-tipped pen. The colour looked violent and angry against the black and white of the paper.

'What do you know about this?' he demanded.

Her stomach churned with sudden anxiety. 'What do I know about what?'

'I warn you, Sky. Don't play games with me. You'll regret it.' His ominous tone promised nothing good.

A mixture of fear and anger tightened her chest. She had no idea what he referred to. No one had

ever spoken to her like this and she didn't like it.
A rush of adrenalin swept through her system.

'Don't you dare talk to me like that!'

'I'll talk to you any damn way I like!' His eyes
flashed dangerously. 'Now, once more: what do you
have to do with this?' He jabbed his finger at the
offending paper. 'And I suggest you tell me
the truth!'

CHAPTER THREE

SKY picked up the newspaper and glanced at the marked item. It wasn't hard to figure out why Mr Chase Montana of the Montana Group was unhappy. The little blurb was bad news for him and his company, mentioning alleged unsavoury business practices and legal action.

She had, however, no idea what it was all about. What she did know was that he was, for all practical purposes, accusing her of having something to do with it. On one level it was a joke, a joke that should make her laugh. She, a mere nature photographer, involved in the defamation of a multinational company? Imagine! Such intrigue! Such glamour!

On another level, it was nothing at all to laugh about and it made her furious.

She forced herself to stay calm and look him straight in the eyes. 'I have no idea what this is about. The first time I set eyes on you was last Friday. The first time I ever heard about the Montana group was when Sean mentioned buying stock a while ago.'

Sean. Did Sean have anything to do with this? He had wanted her to come with him to the cocktail party, which in itself meant nothing, but still. Her mind whirled with sudden confusion. Chase did not like Sean. She'd seen it in his eyes. Could it be that he suspected her of whatever it was because of her association with Sean?

Chase's face was grim. 'Did Sean mention anything concerning these outrageous allegations?' He threw a contemptuous look at the newspaper. 'What did he tell you about the Montana Group?'

Sky stared at him, filled with anger and resentment. 'Nothing. I don't remember. All he talked about was this hotel in Ecuador and how much money he was going to make.'

His eyes narrowed. 'How much money he was going to make?'

'Yes, from the investment.'

'Are you sure?'

'What else? That's what he was talking about! I don't know about anything else! He didn't mention any lawsuit, if that's what you mean. That's what this is all about, isn't it?'

'When was the last time you saw him?'

'Friday, at the party.' She gave a short, humourless laugh. 'Do you think for a moment I'd see him again after the way he treated me?'

He shrugged indifferently. His eyes probed hers and she stared defiantly back at him.

'And I think this is quite enough. I have no intention of submitting myself to your third-degreeing me here, in my own house. Now, get out!'

'When I'm good and ready.'

She turned and walked off, going around the breakfast-bar and into the kitchen, her legs shaking. She couldn't very well throw him out, but she could walk away.

And he could follow, which was what he did. He stood in front of her, very close, his eyes locking with hers, as if he was trying to look into her very soul.

'Has your brother ever mentioned me or my company to you?' he said, his eyes not leaving her face.

The surprise of his question was so great that it overwhelmed all her other feelings—the anger, the fear.

She gaped at him. '*Rocky*?'

'Yes,' he bit out. 'Rocky.'

She began to laugh; she simply couldn't help herself. It was so outrageous she couldn't begin to take it seriously. What could Rocky possibly have to do with a multinational company and a man like Chase? Suspecting easygoing, honest-as-gold Rocky of any sort of foul play was even more ridiculous than accusing her. Rocky had been on a sailing yacht for months, floating around in the Pacific with a bunch of eccentrics. She hadn't seen or talked to him since Christmas. She tried to swallow her laughter. 'You're out of your mind,' she said, and bit hard on her lower lip.

The words hung in the air between them, echoing in the silence. The atmosphere changed, softened. His eyes darkened and the laughter dissolved inside her. A slow, insidious warmth crept through her blood.

'Maybe,' he said softly. 'Maybe I am out of my mind.'

She stood with her back to the counter, mesmerised by his green eyes, his soft, seductive voice. She felt his breath fan her cheek, felt the magnetism of his body so close to hers drawing her closer still. Her blood began to pump and her whole body trembled. She wanted to push him away and run, but her legs would not move. Time stood still and there was no air to breathe. She closed her eyes and then she felt his mouth on hers.

It was like drowning in sensation. His kiss was full of a sensual fire that raced along every nerve-end in her body. She yielded under the warm intensity of his mouth, overwhelmed by a treacherous need welling up from a deep and secret place inside her. Fire. Passion. Urgency. On and on.

Madness.

She struggled for air, for sanity. She could not, would not allow him to overwhelm her like this. She wrenched herself free, suddenly murderously angry—at him, at herself. How could she possibly allow herself to be swept away like this? To feel like this? But as she was asking herself the questions she was well aware that feelings were not controlled by rational thought. Feelings were instinctual. And a very irrational part of her was responding to him with a very primitive need.

'What the hell has gotten into you?' she demanded, her voice husky with emotion.

'The devil,' he said, smiling darkly. 'The devil made me do it.'

And the devil had made her stand there and accept it. She pushed her fingers through her hair and moved away from him with trembling legs, using all her will-power to collect herself and not appear to be a swooning nitwit.

'I don't appreciate this,' she said, struggling for a semblance of dignity, but her voice quavered.

'Oh, yes, you do,' he said with infuriating arrogance. 'You just wish you didn't.' Without another word, he walked right out of the door and was gone.

She leaned weakly against the counter and closed her eyes. One kiss and she was a nervous wreck. This was not good. She didn't want this. She didn't want to be affected like this by a man like Chase Montana. It promised nothing good. She felt an odd sense of foreboding and she covered her face with trembling hands.

Despite the warm summer weather, she shivered.

Sky sat at the kitchen table and read the letter for the third time. It was the kind of letter she normally liked—the kind that came from a company art department with a request to see her portfolio.

Her stomach churned with nerves and she took a gulp of Coke.

Why couldn't she accept this for what it was—a simple request to see her portfolio?

Because she didn't believe for a minute that that was what it was. It was a standard letter, using standard language, but it was printed on Montana Group letterhead, which made all the difference. Alarm bells screamed in her head.

The art department of Chase Montana's company wanted to see her work. If this were simply the way it was, it would be great. Chase Montana's company owned and managed hotels the world over. She could think of a multitude of uses for her work. For one thing, artwork was needed for advertising and publicity, and for the decoration of bedrooms, business offices, lobbies, conference-rooms and more. She took another drink of Coke. What she needed was something stronger—a Scotch and soda, a vodka and tonic. She grimaced. But not at eleven in the morning.

She stared at the letter in front of her and sighed. She didn't trust it. Needless to say, the request had originated with Chase. He had seen her work, if only briefly. He had something in mind, but what? Was he playing games with her? He didn't trust her; she knew that much. She tried not to think about the way he had kissed her, and for what reason.

She could simply ignore the letter, but something inside herself, her fighting spirit, found that solution unacceptable. She was not guilty of anything. She had no reason to be on the defensive. Getting in the door of a large company art department was a great feat all by itself. The competition was fierce. She couldn't let the opportunity just pass her by. Her work was good and she was not afraid to show it. She needed all the chances she could get.

And Chase would know that. Of course he would. What the letter signified was bait. She could pass it by, or bite it.

'Don't play games with me,' Chase had said. 'You'll regret it.' Well, who said he could play games with her?

It was bait, a challenge, a trap. It was danger. Fear mixed with excitement.

Showing her portfolio was a great opportunity. If it was anything else, she wouldn't find out what it was unless she went in and showed her work.

She reached for the phone, called the Montana Group's headquarters in Washington and made an appointment for the following Thursday, eleven in the morning, to meet with the art director.

*   *   *

The art director was a short man with a bald head and piercing blue eyes that seemed to dissect her as he shook hands with her. His manner was formal and off-putting.

It's because the big boss told him to look at my work, thought Sky. He doesn't like to be told who to see, who to hire. Well, she couldn't very well blame him. She presented him with her most charming smile, which, unfortunately, did nothing to melt his reserve.

'All right, show me what you've got,' he said in a tone that barely hid his impatience.

She showed him.

She could almost see the change in him as he studied the mounted images. His body relaxed. The hard features of his face softened. His eyes grew intent. He was looking, really looking, and he liked what he saw.

Sky let out a slow breath, feeling herself relax.

'You have a great eye,' he said, breaking the silence, and the rest of her tension ebbed away. They discussed her work and he told her he wanted to see more.

Sky felt encouraged and elated. The Montana Group was a big company and no doubt this could lead to important work.

Just as they were wrapping things up, a secretary came in and asked her to come with her to Chase's office. Taking a deep breath, Sky followed the woman down a long marble corridor, up in a lift and into an outer office, where she was told to take a seat.

A moment later the door to the inner office opened and Chase himself waved her in. Her pulse quickened at the sight of him—formal and imposing in his dark suit and tie. Yet despite the civilised clothes he emanated a raw male sexuality that pulled at her senses. The memory of his kiss leaped into her mind and she forced it away.

The office was the sort you saw in the movies—vast and luxurious with a huge, empty desk in the middle. Floor-to-ceiling picture windows offered a panoramic view of the Potomac river and original artwork decorated the walls.

'It's time for lunch,' he said, glancing at his watch. 'Hungry?'

She hadn't given it any thought, but now that the question was posed she realised that she was. 'I'll just pick up some fast food on the way home,' she said lightly.

'I thought we'd have lunch together before you leave.'

'Thank you,' she said politely. 'But I'm in a hurry. I have to get ready for my trip to Mexico.'

His eyes met hers and she saw the challenge there, and again her fighting spirit surfaced. She refused to let him think that she was afraid of him or that he made her uncomfortable. She smiled breezily. 'But then, I think I can spare an hour.'

'Thank you,' he said, and there was the faintest trace of mockery in his voice.

He took her down in a private lift and into a company limousine. She'd never been inside a limo before and it was quite an experience to be driven around in such splendour and comfort. There was a bar, a telephone, a small television set and a laptop computer. Everything the busy businessman might need.

'Very impressive,' she said, glancing around. She gestured at the television set. 'I don't suppose that's to keep up with the soaps?'

He stretched out his long legs and leaned back, a spark of humour in his eyes. 'No.'

'I didn't think so. More likely to keep up with the stock market, the financial news and to make sure the world isn't coming to an end while you're on the way somewhere.'

'Wouldn't want to miss it.'

It was a short drive to the restaurant, which was small and had an intimate, European ambience. Had he chosen this on purpose? She felt dread creep through her again and wished she knew what was on his mind.

'Cal likes your work,' he said after they'd given their selections to the waiter.

She frowned. 'How do you know?'

'He called the moment you left his office to come to mine.'

'I see. Yes.' Elation filled her again. 'And he didn't like it because he was told to like it.'

One brow arched. 'Who would have told him to like it?' he said lightly.

'You.'

A faint smile crept around his mouth. 'All I told him was to look.'

As if that weren't enough. Surely the Big Boss didn't make such a demand without certain matters being understood.

'Why?' she asked. 'Why did you want your art director to look at my portfolio? What's behind this?'

He shrugged lightly. 'Because we're always looking for new talent. And your work is good.'

So straightforward, so businesslike. Why didn't she believe that it was as simple as that? She glanced around the room. The atmosphere of the place was relaxed, the patrons not at all the high-energy crowd who came to eat and run. People were taking their time.

Apparently Chase was intent on doing the same. He made easygoing conversation, telling her amusing tales about the hotel business, then went on to ask her casual questions about her work, her life, her family—nothing impertinent, nothing indiscreet, just the normal sort of things that people asked each other when they wanted to get to know each other.

She didn't believe for a moment that the conversation was as casual as he wanted her to think it was. She felt dangerous undercurrents, but was determined not to let him think he made her uneasy. She tried to relax as she talked. After all, she had nothing to hide.

The food was delicious, and she allowed herself to indulge in a scrumptious chocolate dessert. He watched her eat with amusement.

'I haven't seen a woman eat dessert for years,' he said. 'I thought they'd given it up.'

'Not me,' she said breezily.

'When are you leaving for Mexico?' he asked.

'Tomorrow.' She felt a flush of excitement at the thought. She'd done most of her packing already and she couldn't wait to get started.

'I expect Cal will contact you after you get back.'

She bit her lip. 'Thank you,' she said. 'I appreciate your getting me an appointment with him.'

'Don't mention it,' he said evenly and glanced at his watch.

The limousine took them back to the company headquarters and Chase walked with her to the underground parking garage where she'd left her car.

'Enjoy Mexico,' he said as he held the door open for her. She slid behind the steering-wheel.

'Thank you.' She started the engine and drove away.

She didn't know what to make of him. On the surface he was charming and courteous and friendly. Underneath something else was going on. He didn't trust her.

And she didn't trust him.

Six weeks later Sky was in the kitchen filleting four large bass she had caught in the Shenandoah river that morning when the front doorbell rang. Wiping her hands on a towel, she went to open the door.

Chase Montana loomed in front of her.

Her heart lurched. Her stomach tightened. Her whole body trembled.

'Chase?' Her voice croaked. He was the last person she had expected to see. She kept wiping her fishy hands on the towel, feeling her heart doing a ridiculous somersault in her chest. She hadn't seen or heard from him since their lunch in Washington. She'd left for Mexico the next day and her life had been busy. She'd hardly thought of him.

No, that was a lie. She wished she'd hardly thought of him. The truth was that he intruded in her mind at the most unlikely moments. The truth was that she had even dreamed of him while sleeping in a tent in Mexico. This had made her extremely uncomfortable because she had no control over dreams, and she very much liked to stay in control of herself, especially where men were concerned.

He had a bottle of wine in his hand and he looked devastatingly handsome. He wore light grey trousers, a jacket and a shirt and tie—expensive and well-fitting, but nothing particularly spectacular except that it looked spectacular on him. He was that kind of man.

'May I come in?' he asked.

'I'm cleaning fish,' she said inconsequentially.

'Does that mean I can't come in?' He held up the bottle of wine. 'Excellent vintage, woodsy bouquet, crisp. Goes perfect with cleaning raw fish.'

With her bare foot she pushed the door open a little further. 'As you can tell, I wasn't counting on company, but come on in.'

He inclined his head. 'Thank you.'

She closed the door behind him, aware of her own uneasiness, aware of the odd beating of her heart. 'What brings you here?' Maybe he was still trying to figure out if she was somehow involved in that mysterious lawsuit. Maybe he was thinking he could accomplish with wine and charm what he hadn't been able to do with anger and intimidation.

'I'd like to hear about your trip to Mexico. See your photographs. I'm very interested in your photographs.'

Sure he was.

A sudden thought occurred to her. Maybe he was simply checking to see that she had told him the truth about going to Mexico, and that her story about having had an argument with Sean had not been a fabrication to use as an excuse for his departure and her stay-over.

'Checking up to see if I really went?' she asked.

His face was expressionless. 'You wouldn't lie, would you?' he asked smoothly.

'No, I wouldn't,' she said flatly. 'How's the lawsuit coming along?'

She knew she'd made a mistake as soon as she'd said the words. His face turned to stone and his eyes were suddenly cold as he looked at her. A shiver of apprehension ran down her back. The realisation came to her, not for the first time, that it would not be smart to be taken in by his charm, that this was not a man to play games with, not a man you'd want to see angry. His eyes probed hers for what seemed like an eternity while the silence screamed in her ears.

'If you know anything about that lawsuit, Sky,' he said softly, ominously, 'you'd better tell me now.'

She did not like the way he looked at her. Anger rushed through her. He had no right to come into her house and look at her with that cold suspicion. Her heart beat a nervous rhythm and the air seemed to crackle with tension. She looked straight into his cold green eyes.

'I told you before, and I'm telling you now,' she said tightly. 'I don't lie. I don't know anything about that lawsuit and I don't like being distrusted.' Her hands grasped the towel hard. 'I don't know what you want from me and why you are here, but I think you should leave now. I don't need this.' She forced herself to keep looking straight into his eyes.

A silence followed her words and she wondered if he could hear the pounding of her heart.

'I apologise,' he said finally, his eyes not leaving her face. He looked tired now rather than cold.

She wasn't sure what to say. She wasn't sure that his apology was sincere. 'I think you should tell me about that lawsuit.'

'I can't,' he said and the words rang with finality. He held up the bottle of wine in his hand. 'Let's have a drink and forget it.'

She twisted the towel in her hands. 'I don't know if it's something that's easily forgotten. You distrust me, while I have no idea what it's all about. You owe me an explanation.'

'I understand how you feel,' he said, 'but I am in no position to discuss it.' He looked into her eyes, and there was no anger now, no distrust. 'I'm sorry I offended you. Please accept my apologies.'

She wasn't sure what to think of this, but he seemed sincere. She hesitated. 'All right, apologies accepted.' She moved towards the kitchen.

'How did you like Mexico?' he asked as he followed her.

'A photographer's heaven.' She waved at a chair. 'Have a seat. I've got to finish these fish; I shouldn't leave them out.'

'Of course not.' He didn't sit down but stood next to her and glanced at the bass, two of which had been neatly filleted. The remaining two were still in one piece and stared glassily into nothing.

'Where did you get these?'

'I caught them in the river. I went fishing this morning.'

His brows rose fractionally. 'Really?'

'Yes, really,' she said, feeling her sense of humour return. 'I love fishing early in the morning and watching the sun come up.' There was something magical about dawn and it never failed to enthral her.

'And you're cleaning and filleting them yourself. I'm impressed.'

She shrugged lightly. 'There's nothing to it once you know how. I love fish and when I catch it myself it's cheap. Does this gross you out?'

He laughed in obvious amusement. 'No, this does not gross me out. Why don't you let me finish these two for you while you pour us a glass of wine?' He reached up to loosen his tie.

She looked at him sceptically. 'You know how to fillet fish?'

'I do, indeed.' He took off his jacket and rolled up his shirt-sleeves.

She glanced at his brown hands. She could not imagine the man ever having touched raw fish with his bare hands. Gold pens, yes, crystal glasses, yes. Perfumed women, yes. Raw fish, no. Was he trying to confuse her? Mr Montana was a high-powered businessman owning a company operating a string of luxury hotels around the world. Not the type of man you'd expect to find in a remodelled cow barn filleting river bass.

He reached for a tea-towel and tucked it into his belt, then plucked the knife from her nerveless fingers. He took the hapless fish by the tail, slapped it on the chopping-board and made a light incision along the length of the backbone, starting at the head.

All doubt left her as she watched his deft movements. Mr Chase Montana knew how to fillet fish. 'Where did you learn that?' she asked. Probably not in the plantation kitchen.

'The same place I learned how to kill a chicken and butcher a goat.'

'A farm?'

The corner of his mouth twitched. 'I suppose you could call it that.'

The phone rang and she picked up the receiver next to the refrigerator. It was her mother, calling to invite her for Sunday dinner and to tell her she'd received a card from Rocky.

'He's coming home next month!' she said, sounding happy. 'And he wrote he's bringing a girlfriend; can you believe that?'

'Oh, wow,' said Sky. 'He must be serious.' Rocky didn't spend much time in Virginia, and he never brought women with him on his visits home. Not that he had a lack of companionship, she was sure. He was charming and adventurous and owned his own sailing yacht and his blond good looks generated plenty of female attention.

'Maybe a woman will settle him down a little,' said her mother hopefully. Then she laughed at her own folly. 'But I don't think so, really. Can you picture him on dry land in a house with a yard and a couple of kids?'

Sky chuckled. 'No, I can't.'

She was still laughing when she put down the phone.

'You like your mother,' Chase commented.

She nodded. 'Yes. Is that surprising?'

'It's refreshing. It's amazing how many people don't get along with their parents. I'm tired of hearing people blame all their failures on their parents.'

Sky found some wine glasses—cheap, French bistro variety. 'Not me. My parents are great. What about yours?'

'No complaints, at least not since I grew up. My father died four years ago. My mother is wonderful. She recently remarried.'

'And her husband? You get along with him?'

'Superbly.' He put the fillets on the tray of ice and washed his hands.

She poured the wine and handed him a glass. 'Well, aren't we lucky? We should have a toast. Here's to all good parents.'

They clinked glasses. 'What do you like about yours?' he asked.

She sat down at the kitchen table. 'Lots of stuff.' She grinned. 'Mostly that they allowed me to run wild and free as a kid.'

He sat down across from her. 'And what did you do running wild and free?'

'I played with turtles, kept rabbits, climbed trees and was forever filthy. My brother and I had a canoe and we spent hours on the river, fishing and swimming and generally fooling around. Of course I was lucky. My father is a forest ranger and thought this was exactly what we ought to be doing. My mother is a pre-school teacher and still a kid at heart herself and is a consummate believer in free expression.'

'Sounds like you had a great childhood.'

'Oh, yes, the best. It didn't necessarily prepare me for a more normal, ordered lifestyle as an adult.' Which was why she was having so much trouble with architects, business consultants and computer analysts, of course. Initially they found her amusing, a little untamed. She was much happier crawling through mud trying to get eye-level with a frog than out dancing in heels. She climbed rocks, waded waist-deep through murky water, hid for hours high up in trees, all for the sake of a good shot of some lower form of life. After a while they could not quite take it and set out to tame her.

At which point she would tell them to take a hike.

After which she would cry her heart out and wonder why she was always getting involved with the wrong men, and where were the right ones?

The right ones, of course, were crawling through swamps and climbing trees, not sitting in leather chairs in fancy business offices dressed in Italian suits.

'Do you want a normal, ordered lifestyle?' Chase asked, looking at her intently over the rim of his glass.

She wondered suddenly what kind of wife a man like Chase Montana would look for, if he were looking for a wife at all. He'd need an efficient woman with a well-organised, regulated life. A woman who would know how to manage a large house and how to entertain. A woman who would always be dressed correctly, and certainly never in a dress with parrots on it. A woman who spoke only after she'd thought about what to say first, not someone who spouted off without thinking, offending people in the process. That sort of thing could be very dangerous in Chase's circles.

She thought of the kind of life that woman would lead and it sounded to her like death. Involuntarily, she gave a little shiver.

'If I wanted a more ordered life, I would be sitting in a studio nine to five and taking family portraits all day.'

He took a drink of his wine. 'And that doesn't appeal to you?'

'I hate portrait photography.' She grimaced. 'Of course, I was never any good at it.'

'Not exactly the wild and free variety of photography,' he acknowledged.

'I studied it in college as part of the total curriculum. I'd be all set up, having my victims sitting ramrod-straight and producing these sickly stilted smiles and all I wanted to do was dance the hula or do something else outrageous to make them fall all over each other so I could get a fun candid shot.' She chuckled. 'Once I actually did that. I made some horrific face. First they froze in shock and their eyes popped out, then they completely disintegrated. That's when I took the shot.'

'How did it come out?'

She grinned. 'I thought it was great. The family loved it, and later I sold it to a family life magazine for a hundred dollars. I'd never felt so rich in my life. I was still in college.' She took a sip of wine. 'I saw a portrait of you and your family in your office,' she said impulsively.

He nodded. 'Stunningly formal, I believe. We all looked dead as doornails.'

She laughed. 'But very proper and very handsome.'

'I remember when it was taken. I was plotting an act of defiance, but didn't quite make it in time.' He nodded at the fish fillets. 'What are you going to do with them now? Freeze them?'

'Yes.' She came to her feet and got out plastic wrap from a cupboard. 'Let me take care of them now and then I'll show you my pictures of Mexico.'

The terrible thing was that she actually enjoyed talking to him, this man who wore expensive suits and spent his days in an opulent office and who most certainly never climbed trees. This was not good. She didn't want to be taken in by his charm. She wanted to dislike him. She *did* dislike him. He wasn't at all her type of man—she'd learned that from hard experience. His interests centred on profit margins, the price of stock and building big hotels in rainforests. He had intriguing green eyes, true, and interesting stories to tell, but that was all.

And he liked her photographs. She could tell just by the way he looked at them—with genuine interest and admiration. He sat next to her on one of the sofas as he studied her Mexico photos that lay spread out on the large coffee-table—the ones she had selected out of the many rolls of film she had taken.

'They're magnificent. Cal said you have a wonderful eye and I see what he means.'

'Thank you.' She felt a rush of emotion—a happiness beyond the normal pleasure she usually felt at someone's compliments. She was aware of how close he was sitting. How easy it would be to touch him. She stared at his hand holding one of the pictures, seeing the brown fingers, the neat square fingernails. And suddenly came the urge to touch that hand, to feel the warmth and strength of it, the urge to draw him closer and kiss him. Oh, God. She swallowed and dragged her gaze away from him and focused on one of the pictures.

He picked up another photo to examine it closer. 'I don't understand how someone could possibly not take your work seriously.'

He was referring to Sean without mentioning his name. She shrugged. 'I don't make a ton of money and to some people that's what counts, that's the only validation.'

'A pretty cynical view.'

'Yes, it is. But some people feel that way.'

'Does it bother you?'

She shrugged. 'It was worse when I was really struggling in the beginning and could hardly keep myself going financially. My confidence was very fragile then, but I'm all right now. I feel good about my work, and I'm getting good assignments. I had a series on exhibit at the Benedict gallery in Washington last fall that was very successful.' She pointed at the wall. 'That series of shots over there on the far left.'

He nodded. 'I noticed that one last time. The one called *Hope*.'

'Yes. It sold to an environmental organisation. It's hanging in their offices.' It was a series of ten images, each picturing a piece of ugliness redeemed by new life, among them a mangled, abandoned car wreck with a cat and her new-born kittens nestling in the driver's seat; a rotting mattress sprouting colourful weeds; a heap of rusting scrap metal with a row of white ducks on it, preening.

She asked him to stay for dinner and eat some of the bass. She had not intended to invite him. The invitation just sort of came out of her mouth of its own volition.

They had the fish with brown rice and stir-fried wild mushrooms she had collected the day before, and salad. The wine he had brought was delicious and complemented the meal perfectly.

He came to his feet soon after coffee. 'I had better be off,' he said. 'Thank you for a wonderful meal.'

She walked him to the door and opened it. He smiled down at her, meeting her eyes. 'I enjoyed this very much,' he said.

Her heart began to race. 'So did I,' she said, hoping her voice sounded steady.

He reached out, drew her close against him and determinedly put his mouth on hers.

CHAPTER FOUR

IT WAS a shattering kiss and Sky was not prepared for its impact. The moment his arms came around her, the moment his strong mouth touched hers, her body flushed with a heat that rendered her immobile. His mouth was warm and sensuous, his tongue a magical instrument of pleasure—teasing, tantalising. Time stood still. He pressed her closer against him and every inch of her body made contact with his. Her every cell seemed to dance with delight.

All her resistance to him, all her denials and rational thinking had nothing to do with this—this flaring of instant connection, as if her body had been waiting for this, preparing for this, responding now with joyful abandon. All her thoughts and decisions turned meaningless faced with the instinctive response of her senses.

She felt hypnotised. She was in a delicious trance, revelling in his touch, the heat of his mouth, the warm male scent of him. She responded to his kiss with an elemental urgency she had no power to control, didn't want to control.

'You weren't meant for a manless life, you know that?' he whispered against her mouth.

His words brought her back to the fringes of sanity. Her rational mind struggled out of oblivion. She registered time, place, the fact that she had just been kissed senseless and had actually enjoyed it and responded to it.

She moaned and strained against his hold, pulling away her mouth with an effort.

He did not retain her, but let go of her without moving away from her. She wanted to tell him to stay away from her, that she didn't trust him, that she was not interested in an affair with him. That she didn't want him to kiss her ever again. But the words did not come from her mouth.

He smiled a slow, utterly seductive smile as he surveyed her face. He touched a gentle finger to her lips. 'Don't say a thing,' he said softly. 'Goodnight, Sky.'

He turned and was gone.

She sagged down on one of the sofas and buried her face in her hands. What did he think he was trying to prove? That he had power over her? That he could control her?

And why was she feeling the way she was feeling? Was she fooling herself pretending she wasn't attracted to him?

It was lust, plain and simple. The man had sex appeal. The man knew how to kiss. The man had magic eyes and his voice made her heart drum a dance tune. Of course she was attracted to him.

She moaned into her hands.

But all that was nothing but shallow physical appeal. It had nothing to do with the real thing.

The real thing.

She didn't want a shallow, meaningless affair, no matter how exciting it might be while it lasted. In the end the price would be too high, no matter how sophisticated she thought she might be. Deep down she would always be that unsophisticated, romantic idealist who wanted the real thing—promises and commitments and dreams to share. None of these could she expect from a man like Chase Montana. She knew that. She understood that. Then why did she allow herself to feel this way?

Because I'm a stupid fool, she thought. Because for some perverted reason I fall in love with the wrong men. Because I have this crazy, unfathomable need for self-destruction.

But no matter how much she told herself that she wasn't interested in a money-hungry molester of rainforests, she kept thinking about him, dreaming about him. It was as if some spell had been put on her and she couldn't get him out of her mind. She thought of him as she hiked through the woods in search of picture material. She thought of him at night as she lay in her loft staring up into the rafters. There was something elusive about him, something that didn't quite click with the image which he presented to her—something quite intriguing and disturbing.

She certainly hadn't expected him to know how to fillet fish. The thought made her smile.

'Where did you learn that?' she'd asked.

'The same place I learned how to kill a chicken and to butcher a goat.'

'A farm?'

'I suppose you could call it that.'

Like a computer, her brain reproduced the conversation. 'You could call it that. You could call it that. You could call it that.'

There was something about that sentence that struck her. Obviously the place had not been an ordinary farm. Then what had it been? What kind of place did a man like Chase go to and learn to butcher goats?

'It scares me,' she told her friend Beth who had come by for a visit, bearing a gift of chocolate cheesecake. 'I feel so out of control.'

'Why is that?' Beth pushed her long dark hair over her shoulder and forked a piece of cake into her mouth.

'I don't know.' Sky made a helpless gesture. 'He has this way about him, as if he's got me caught on a hook and he's reeling me in like a damned fish, and all I can do is throw myself into helpless contortions.'

Beth nearly choked on her cake. 'I love your image,' she spluttered. 'It's so...so *vivid*.'

'Thank you,' said Sky drily, but a smile escaped her as she looked at Beth's grinning face. Then she sighed. 'I don't know what to do!' she wailed. 'Tell me what to do!'

Beth grimaced. 'No way. Ask Dear Abby.'

Sky gave her a disparaging look. 'Some friend you are. Here I am, confused, angst-ridden, desperate and you won't even give me any advice.'

Beth groaned. 'OK, OK, let's look at this rationally. What we have here is a wealthy, sophisticated businessman with a historic mansion and a lot of sex appeal who's coming on to you. No offence, Sky, but may we say that his regular taste of women probably does not stretch to include nature photographers who run around in muddy jeans and boots? Add to that that he's been suspecting you of mysterious crimes, but won't tell you what it's all about. First he's suspicious and offensive, now he's charming and seductive. The guy wants something from you, Sky. I don't like it.'

Sky sighed. 'I was afraid you'd see it that way.'

'Is there any other way to see it?'

Sky made a face. ' "Hope springs eternal". I was hoping you'd come up with a more positive interpretation of the facts. This is so depressing.'

'Have another piece of cheesecake,' offered Beth. 'It's excellent medicine for troubled minds.'

'Yeah, the cholesterol will clog my arteries and I'll die and all my problems will be over.'

'Shut up and eat,' said Beth, putting another piece in front of her.

Sky made a face at her. 'What am I going to do after you leave? Who will I talk to when I have a problem?'

'Me,' said Beth. 'On the phone. You'll have astronomical bills, but it will still be cheaper than therapy.'

They talked about Beth's upcoming move to an Indian reservation in North Dakota, where Kevin would manage a local medical clinic and Beth would teach at the elementary school. All their friends had told them they were crazy to move to such a remote location, but they were not to be discouraged.

After Beth had left, Sky sat at the kitchen table and started making preparations for the farewell party she and several other friends were organising for Beth and Kevin. It was scheduled for the coming Saturday and Sky had offered her house for the occasion.

She found a piece of paper and made a shopping list. She needed charcoal for the grill, ice for the drinks.

She needed divine inspiration for her tormented heart.

Sky was out on the terrace and she watched the festivities with satisfaction. It was a good party. People were everywhere, inside and out, replete with barbecued chicken, potato salad and conversation. Surrounded by friends, food and good cheer, Sky felt in excellent spirits. Much of her working life was spent alone and she enjoyed having her friends around at times like this. She went inside to pour herself another glass of wine and the breath caught in her throat.

Chase was standing in the living-room, talking with Kevin. He was leaning casually against one of the rough wooden beams that supported the sleeping-loft, a glass of wine in his hand. Her heart began to race. Damn! What was he doing here? She watched his face and all she could think of was the way he had kissed her the last time he'd been here and she grew warm with the memory of it. All she could do was just stand there like a woman possessed and stare at him.

'What's the matter with you?' asked Beth, waving a hand in front of her eyes. 'You're looking glassy-eyed.'

Startled, Sky shook her head. 'Nothing.'

Beth glanced into the direction she'd been looking. 'That's him, isn't it?' she asked. 'Did you invite him?'

'No.' She felt a helpless sense of inevitability. She moved further into the room, towards him.

Chase looked up. It was hard to read his eyes. 'Just passing by,' he said, which was a blatant lie, and they both knew it. Her barn was tucked away deep in the countryside and no one ever 'just passed by'.

She smiled sweetly. 'Of course.' Short of making a scene, she couldn't very well tell him to leave in front of everyone.

He was dressed in casual clothes and looked perfectly comfortable, perfectly at home. It was a perfectly uncomfortable realisation. His presence added a breathless quality to the atmosphere, at least for her. She turned and walked away, but his eyes seemed to follow her everywhere. Whenever she happened to look in his direction, his green gaze was directed at her.

She was doing it again. She was falling for a man who was all wrong for her. And, what was worse, she didn't even trust his motives.

She moved around in a daze, talking automatically, filling plates of food without thinking, smiling mindlessly. There was music and laughter and everyone was having a great time, but all of it seemed to be happening as if at a distance, as if she weren't really part of it.

Then someone in the living-room let out a cry of fear and suddenly the talk and laughter abated. Suddenly everything was very real. Everyone stared in frozen horror at Beth. Her eyes were bulging. Her hands grabbed her throat and she was turning blue. Sky's heart slammed against her ribs and she leaped from behind the breakfast-bar and hurled herself across the room.

She wasn't fast enough. Action erupted in the room. Chase dragged Beth out of the chair, encircled her with his arms and pushed his fists into her sternum. Something shot out of her throat and she drew in air in a tortured gasp. Tears streamed down her face as she gulped for more air. Chase released her into Kevin's arms.

Sky sagged limply on to a floor cushion, watching Kevin hold Beth in his arms. He looked ashen. It had happened so fast, and was over so quickly, it was difficult to take in. A minute of panic and confusion, fast action, and then nothing.

As if on cue, the talking and laughing continued, be it with a nervous tone. Seeing death so narrowly being escaped was a nerve-racking experience, and one no one wished to linger over it.

Chase was the hero of the evening, the great rescuer, the evictor of lodged peanuts. He was great, they told Sky. Who was he? Where had she found him? He was so good-looking and sophisticated and sexy. He had such fascinating stories! He was such an exciting man! By the end of the evening it was quite clear that if she wanted to get rid of Chase Montana she could forget about getting support from her friends. As far as they were concerned, he was the man for her, no doubt about it.

It was well after one before people started leaving. Sky hugged Kevin, then Beth as she said goodbye.

'Be happy, Beth,' she said, hugging her hard.

'You too,' whispered Beth. There were tears in her eyes. She gestured at the coffee-table. 'There are some pictures I found when I sorted through my stuff. I thought you would want them.' She bit her lip, glancing over Sky's shoulder in the direction of the sofa on which Chase was still comfortably ensconced. 'I wish you'd find someone again, Sky.' Then she turned and rushed out of the door without looking back.

Sky swallowed at the lump in her throat and closed the door. The house seemed awfully silent and she felt suddenly overwhelmed by a sense of desolation. Without Beth and Kevin there'd be a hole in her life. They'd both known Josh and were a link to her past—a past that seemed to grow ever dimmer.

She glanced around the room. Everybody had helped clean up and there was nothing to do. She wished there were, just so that she could keep herself busy and Chase would get the message and leave.

Chase was watching her. 'I shouldn't have crashed your party,' he stated, but there was no apology in his voice.

'I'm glad you were here,' she said. It was the truth, but she felt the line being reeled in a little closer. He patted the seat next to him.

'Sit down,' he said.

She did as he suggested, noticing the envelope Beth had left on the table. She picked it up. It wasn't sealed. There were two snapshots inside and her heart turned over as she looked at them.

They were pictures of her and Josh, amateur snapshots taken by Beth, or maybe Kevin. One showed her and Josh sitting on a wooden dock, fishing in the rain, close together, arms around each other, grinning like fools. The other showed Josh sitting with his back against a tree, and her stretched out with her head in his lap. They were both sound asleep. A blue butterfly had settled on her hair.

They looked so young and innocent. She looked at the pictures with a terrible longing, a longing for something precious that had been lost and would never be found again. In some ways these two people in the pictures were strangers, and she smiled with a painful nostalgia.

'Sky?'

Chase's voice startled her. She had forgotten he was there. He gave her a curious smile. 'You were so still. It looked as if you were in a trance.'

She swallowed and shook her head.

He glanced at the photos in her hand. 'You seem very young there.'

'Nineteen.'

'Was he your boyfriend?'

She bit her lip. 'No. My husband.' She saw the flare of surprise in his eyes.

'I didn't know,' he said.

'I didn't tell you.'

'What was his name?'

'Josh. Joshua Milliken. I kept my own name.' Even then, romantic or not, she had been fiercely independent. When she was going to make a name for herself as a photographer it was going to be as Sky Malone.

There was a silence as she kept looking at the photos. 'What happened?' he asked at last.

'He died.' Her voice was toneless. 'Seven months after we were married. A head-on collision with a drunk in a big Mercedes Benz.' Her hands trembled and the pictures dropped to the table. Even now, after all these years, it shook her to have to tell the gruesome truth.

'I'm sorry,' he said softly.

'It was a long time ago,' she said, as if that made it any less of a tragedy. 'I look at these pictures and I feel so old.'

'Old?' He smiled a little. 'How old are you?'

'Twenty-seven.'

'Not so old.'

She smiled now too. 'No, not really.' She tapped the pictures. 'But here I was a lifetime younger.'

'And very much in love.'

'Yes.' She gave a half-smile. 'He was my first boyfriend and I never wanted anybody else. Can you believe that? I was sixteen when I met him and I knew he was it, period.'

'Sometimes it's as simple as that,' he said, his eyes meeting hers. Something vibrated between them and her heart lurched. She lowered her gaze and shook her head, as if denying some unspoken words.

'It will never be simple again,' she said quietly.

'Tell me about it,' he urged.

She smiled wryly. 'It's not a very exciting story.'

'Tell me anyway.' He leaned back against the sofa and waited expectantly.

'We worked on the high-school paper together. Josh was a year ahead of me in school and we met when I was sixteen and he seventeen. We were inseparable from the start.' She paused. 'A year later he went away to college to study journalism. My parents thought it would be good for us not to be together so much. They thought I was too young. They hoped distance would create more objectivity and that the romance would peter out.' She looked down at her hands, smiling.

'It didn't,' Chase stated.

'No. Being apart was agony. We couldn't stand it. All we wanted was to be together. So after I graduated I went to the same college and we were together again. We were married in the spring of my first year. We had a wedding in the woods, by a small pond, very romantic. We wrote our own vows, very sixties-ish. We went back to college and lived in an attic apartment with a slanted ceiling. We planned and we dreamed.' She bit her lip. Suddenly it was hard to go on.

'It all seems so long ago now,' she said finally. 'Sometimes it doesn't even seem it's me I'm talking about—as if it all happened in another lifetime, to somebody else.'

'Why is that?'

'We were both so young and idealistic. We had so many dreams and hopes.'

Tears suddenly flooded her eyes. 'Oh, damn,' she muttered. 'I'm sorry.'

'Don't be,' he said. 'What were you dreaming about?'

She managed a watery smile. 'We were going to save the world, what else?' she said, her voice containing a note of humour.

He smiled back at her in recognition of her self-derision. 'And how were you planning to do that?'

'Josh wanted to be a writer and travel the world and I wanted to be a photographer and travel the world. Together we would make up this fantastic team, going on adventurous trips to all kinds of obscure corners of the globe. We'd write riveting travel books and fascinating photo-articles for classy magazines and show everybody how beautiful the earth is and how important it is to take care of it.' She bit her lip.

'Ah, the idealism of the young,' he said softly, but there was no mockery in his voice. 'What about your dreams and hopes now?'

She shrugged. 'I still hope my photos show something, mean something to people.' She gave a lop-sided smile. 'I don't think in grand terms of saving the earth, but I do hope to travel more and maybe produce a photo book that might help in some small way.' She looked down at her hands. 'Only I don't have anyone to share this with, like before. That was the beautiful part of it all—to have someone to dream with.' She smiled through her tears. 'I feel like such a sentimental slob.' She wiped her eyes. 'I haven't cried about this for a long time.'

He put his arms around her, saying nothing. She didn't resist. It felt good.

After a while, he stirred, releasing her reluctantly. 'I'd better go,' he said, his mouth curving in a rueful smile.

She didn't want him to go. She wanted the comfort of his warm body, the strength of his arms around her. No, it was insanity. A moment of weakness would not give her dreams. Chase was not the right man.

His mouth brushed across hers.

'Never give up hope,' he said.

Later she lay in bed thinking how easy it would have been for her to ask him to stay. How easy it would have been to say yes if he had asked her.

He hadn't asked.

*   *   *

Two days later he called her. She had never heard
his voice over the phone and it sounded quite imposing—a voice that commanded an attentive ear.

'How would you like an assignment in the
Caribbean?' he asked. 'All expenses paid, of
course.'

How would she like an assignment in the
Caribbean? Her head was suddenly light with excitement. She'd love to go to the Caribbean! Of
course she would! She closed her eyes and
swallowed an enthusiastic reply. Mr Chase Montana
of the Montana Group was offering her an assignment. Normally she was not a suspicious
person, but now, in the circumstances, she could
only wonder what was behind it.

Don't fall for it! said the sensible part of herself.
She straightened her spine and shifted the receiver
to her other ear.

'What kind of assignment are we talking about?'
she asked, willing her voice to sound calm, as if
this were merely a run-of-the-mill discussion. As if
she had offers of this nature on a regular basis.

'We need pictures for a potential new site—the
scenery, the wildlife, et cetera. They'll be part of a
project presentation. It's on St Barlow, a tiny little
island. I'll show you on a map.'

'Are you intending to build a tourist hotel?' She
heard the faint undertone of censure in her own
voice.

'No, not a hotel, possibly a nature resort. We're
merely exploring the possibility right now, that's
all. We research a lot more places than we ever use.'

A nature resort. This sounded better. The idea
of her getting herself involved in the irresponsible

development of a tiny island was not appetising. She heard the rustling of paper, as if he was turning pages.

'The problem is, we'll have to go soon.'

Her heart crash-landed at her feet. '*We*?' she asked.

'Yes. I'll have to talk to the government people and local entrepreneurs, do a feasibility study. Are you at all booked for next week and the three weeks after that?'

She had no professional assignments, but Rocky was coming home with his girlfriend. She hadn't seen him since Christmas. Maybe he'd still be here after she got back, if she went. Rocky's plans and schedules were not known for their rigidity and accuracy, nor was his life in general.

Four weeks on a tiny island with Chase was a recipe for disaster. The image of herself dangling on a fishing-line being reeled in was frightfully real. She felt a sense of doom take over. 'I'll have to think about this,' she said, her voice indicating a calm control she didn't in the least possess.

'Of course,' he said smoothly, as if he didn't know that she was foaming at the bit, as if he didn't know this was a fantastic assignment for her, one she would ordinarily accept with a whoop of triumph. 'Let me give you some idea of the island charms,' he went on.

The island had many, according to Chase—idyllic, palm-fringed beaches, coral reef full of magical marine life, a wild, rocky north-eastern coast, a volcanic mountain covered with rainforest. Wildlife included a species of parrot endemic on the island as well as other rare species of birds, colourful lizards, iguanas and more. She listened with mounting excitement as he spoke.

'Now, let me give you the details,' he said.

The details included a high fee on top of all travel and lodging expenses. She suppressed a moan of frustration. Why was he doing this to her? He was making it impossible for her to say no.

He didn't *want* her to say no. But why? He must want her to go to the island for a reason. There had to be an ulterior motive. Did he still harbour suspicions about her? If he didn't trust her, how then could she trust him?

She took a deep breath. She was going to play it cool, not be too eager. 'I'm curious,' she said casually. 'There are thousands of photographers. Why me?'

'Because I want you.'

The words shivered in the air.

Because he wanted her. She said nothing and the silence was unnerving.

'I admire your work,' he went on. 'I know what you are capable of. It makes excellent business sense for the company to offer you this assignment.' It sounded eminently believable, eminently rational. She wished she could believe that that was all there was to it, but she could not escape feeling an odd sense of foreboding.

She pressed her eyes shut. 'I appreciate your confidence.'

'When you make up your mind,' he went on, 'let me know. If you don't want the job, we'll have to find someone else and we have very little time left. Here, let me give you my number.'

'I have the number.'

'Not the one for my apartment.'

She grabbed a pen and wrote it down dutifully. 'I didn't know you had an apartment,' she said, surprised.

'The house is the family's house and besides it's too far out for a regular commute. My mother and her husband live there most of the year.'

'I see.'

'The company sometimes uses it for entertainment,' he elaborated. 'Excuse me for a moment.' She heard him say something to another person, then he was back on the line. 'All right, give me a call by tomorrow noon and let me know what you've decided.' He said goodbye and hung up.

Sky got up and walked around in a daze. Curiosity mingled with her apprehension. She closed her eyes and felt his lips on her mouth and her heartbeat quickened. She moaned. Beth's words echoed in her head.

'First he's suspicious and offensive, now he's charming and seductive. The guy wants something from you, Sky. I don't like it.'

Danger. Excitement. Opportunity.

Later that night she lay in bed on her sleeping-loft and stared up into the rafters.

She wanted the job.

Of course she did. She needed the job and she couldn't afford to say no to such a fantastic opportunity. It was a job that could generate many others. It would be a valuable addition to her portfolio. Lovely visions danced in her head—aquamarine waters, exotic tropical flowers, colourful birds and butterflies, palm trees fluttering in the tradewind breezes.

She wanted the job.

No, she did not want the job. She didn't want to be beholden to Chase Montana. She could not afford to be drawn closer into his circle of power and influence. He frightened her with his charm, his green eyes, his sexy mouth.

He was playing games with her. She could not afford to play games with her heart and her emotions.

Absolutely not. He was not her type. He was too handsome, too sure of himself, too dangerous. His company destroyed rainforests. She didn't trust his motives, whatever they were.

It was unconscionable to be involved with someone who destroyed rainforests and crassly invaded the lives and culture of defenceless people.

The terrible thing was that she was falling for him, for the gleam in his eyes, for the mysteries behind them. There was more to Chase Montana than met the eye, and she couldn't help but be hopelessly intrigued, attracted, enamoured. She couldn't help the treacherous sense of need and yearning she felt when he kissed her. She couldn't help that, in spite of all that, she still didn't trust him.

She buried her face in the pillow and moaned.

Love would never be simple again, as it had been so many years ago when she had loved Josh. And never again would dreams be so beautiful and delicious.

'Oh, Josh,' she whispered into the silence. 'Why did you have to die?' But her mind could not call up Josh's face. All she saw behind her closed lids was Chase.

At three minutes before twelve the next morning, fortified with three cups of strong coffee, she called Chase's office. Her hand shook. She was a nervous wreck.

The secretary connected her immediately, asking no questions, and a moment later Chase's deep voice came over the line.

'I've decided I'd like to take on the assignment we discussed yesterday,' she said in her most professional business voice. Yet she felt as if she was diving off a high cliff and she was falling, tumbling down like a ragdoll, over and over, out of control.

I am out of control, she thought, and pressed her head against the glass of the kitchen window, fighting panic. I'm out of control.

CHAPTER FIVE

'EXCELLENT,' Chase said in equally calm tones. 'Let's talk schedule.'

They talked schedule. Unfortunately a crisis had occurred in one of their Far East hotels, he said, and it was crucial that he make a quick trip to Thailand.

A quick trip to Thailand. As if it were New York or Chicago. Sky wished she could so casually mention quick trips to exotic places. She could hear herself now. I can't make it to dinner on Saturday. I'm leaving on a short assignment to the Central Africa Republic—the elephants, you know. No, next month won't work either. I'll be in India shooting leopards.

Chase said he was leaving tonight and he would not be able to come to the island right away. She'd have to go on her own.

She let out a sigh of relief—slowly, so that he wouldn't hear it over the phone. She'd be delighted to travel there on her own. The less she saw of him the better. Her nerves needed the rest.

'No problem,' she said calmly.

'I'm not sure when I'll get there—probably the following Friday or Saturday.' He sounded so businesslike, so perfectly professional, it was hard to believe he was the same man who had held her in his arms and kissed her senseless mere days ago. No, she was just fooling herself thinking that—it wasn't hard to believe at all. Even his businesslike voice had that sexy, sensuous quality that slid straight into her system and quickened her pulse. She closed her eyes, pushing away disturbing thoughts, and concentrated on his words.

'I have some paperwork for you—contract, tickets, map, and a cheque for your advance, and the keys for the car. You won't need one for the house.'

'What house? What car?'

'My house on the island, and my car. You'll need to stay somewhere and you'll need transportation.'

Yes, of course.

'Mrs Drakes is the woman who keeps an eye on the place when no one is there,' he continued. 'She'll take care of things while you're there. She does the cooking and cleaning and whatever you need.'

She'd never had anyone do her cooking and cleaning. It sounded like an idea she could probably get used to. 'Sounds good to me,' she said.

'Now, I'll have to ask you a favour. I'm flying out tonight, but it was rather last-minute and I have to go back to the house to pick up something I need. I'll be there about four this afternoon. I'll bring the paperwork. Can you come to the house and meet me there? We'll discuss the assignment a little further and deal with whatever questions you may have, and I'll give you the car keys. They're at the house.'

Could she please come to the den of the tiger? Sky closed her eyes, feeling a sense of fatalism take over.

Sure, why not?

*   *   *

The woman who opened the large front door to the plantation house was small, slim and had delicate female curves in all the right places. Her eyes were very dark brown, her hair straight, glossy black. Her features were Eurasian and her accent British. She wore loose black trousers and a simple blouse of amethyst silk and she was stunningly beautiful.

'Hello,' she said, and smiled.

'Hi. I'm here to see Chase,' said Sky, wishing she'd put on something a bit more sophisticated than her denim shorts and pink T-shirt. 'He asked me to come by and pick up some papers.' A heap of luggage lay in the marble entrance hall.

'Oh, please come in. He isn't here, but he'll be here soon. Something must have delayed him.'

Sky moved inside. 'I'm Sky Malone,' she said, and held out her hand.

'I'm Michelle Harding.' She gestured at the pile of expensive suitcases. 'I've just come home. Excuse the mess. Mrs Lumpkins is making me some tea. Would you like a cup while you wait?'

'Yes, thank you.' She followed Michelle into the sitting-room, which gleamed with grandeur, yet had a warm, inviting look in spite of the imposing pieces of antique furniture. Plants and flowers added life and cheer, and stacks of books and magazines gave the room a lived-in look. An exquisitely carved wooden chess set was perched on a side-table, a game in progress.

'Please have a seat.' Michelle waved in the direction of a sofa and chairs arranged around a square coffee-table adorned with a bouquet of fragrant yellow roses. 'I'll tell Mrs Lumpkins you're here. I'll only be a moment.'

'I've just come home'. She lived here, then. Michelle then was the woman of the lovely bedroom and the wardrobe full of beautiful clothes. 'This is my—er—sister's room', Chase had said.

Sister, my foot, she thought. The family portrait in the study had not shown a daughter, nor parents who could have produced a daughter with Asian features. And Michelle spoke with a foreign accent; she hadn't grown up with Chase who spoke with the faint but elegant southern lilt of the Virginia landed gentry.

Absently she picked up a magazine that lay on the table. It had the Montana Group logo on the front and was an in-house publication for the company's investors. Photographs showed luxury hotels, exquisitely laid-out grounds complete with golf courses and tennis courts and olympic-size swimming-pools. She glanced through it, not finding much of interest, until her eyes caught the name Ecuador. A short bulletin informed the reader that the Ecuador project was on hold. Objections had been raised over the size of the hotel and the Ecuadorian government was reassessing the situation. She grinned to herself, feeling a flash of smug satisfaction. Good! Her instincts had been right.

A woman came into the room with a tray of tea things, followed by Chase who'd apparently just arrived. Her heart turned over as she saw his tall figure come through the door. He looked imposing and handsome in his immaculate business suit—a man of the world. A man in control.

In control.

Suspicion reared its ugly head. What did this man want with her?

'Hi,' she said with as little expression as she could manage.

'Sorry I wasn't here,' he said and settled himself on the sofa next to her. 'I appreciate your coming here. I wanted to see you before you left.'

'No problem.' She wished he'd sat down in a chair across from her. He was too close for comfort, but there was nothing she could do about it.

He opened his briefcase and took out some paperwork. 'Here you go: contract, tickets, address, et cetera.'

She took the contract and began to read it carefully. It was nothing out of the ordinary, no devious clauses or anything she objected to. There was no reason whatsoever not to sign it.

So why was she hesitating? She stared at the paper.

'Everything in order?'

'Yes.'

'What's wrong?' He sensed her trepidation. Of course he did. He was a smart man. A smart man who wouldn't tell her why he had suspected her, and of what.

She looked at him, fighting sudden anger. 'I wish I knew,' she said. 'I wish I knew why you're so interested in my taking this assignment. It has something to do with that lawsuit, doesn't it?'

The magic word. His face stiffened marginally and his eyes grew expressionless. 'No one is forcing you to go,' he said evenly.

No. And on the surface everything was a straightforward business deal. Nothing funny, nothing fishy, everything above board. Nothing suspicious in the contract.

'You've tried to make me think that you're interested in me and that perhaps you want me on the island for more...personal reasons, but I don't buy that, either. I'm not stupid.' She picked up a pen and signed her name in the space provided on the contract and handed it back to him, looking straight into his eyes. 'Just so you know I know.'

One eyebrow rose in question. 'And what does that mean?'

Her heart pounded. 'It means don't play games with me, or you'll regret it,' she said, echoing the warning he'd once made to her. It sounded so determined, so in control. As if she actually thought she had any defence against him. Well, she had to pretend she had.

Something flashed in his eyes, but before he could say anything in return Michelle entered the living-room. 'Ah, there you are,' she said to Chase, and smiled. 'Tea. Good! I'm parched.'

'Have you met my sister?' Chase asked and his mouth twitched.

'We've met,' said Michelle, and she draped herself elegantly in a chair. She glanced from Sky to Chase and back to Sky. She laughed. 'He didn't tell you, did he?'

'Didn't tell me what?'

'That we don't share the same gene pool. My father is British and my mother was Hong Kong Chinese. She died when I was little. My father married his mother three months ago. He has whole-heartedly accepted me as a sister, which is very nice, but it confuses people.'

Three months ago. Sky made a quick calculation. That had been shortly before she'd met

Chase at the investors' cocktail party. *'This is my—er—sister's room'*, he'd said. At the time he must have still been trying out the sister bit. She remembered the gleam in his eyes. Of course there had been absolutely no reason to explain this sister thing to a stranger. Having accidentally stowed away in his house, she, Sky Malone, had been a stranger.

Michelle glanced over at Chase, then back at Sky. 'He enjoys confusing people. I assume it's a psychological quirk left over from his rather—er—unconventional teenage years.' She smiled at Sky. 'He probably didn't tell you about that either, did he?'

Chase glanced meaningfully at his watch. 'How about that cup of tea?' he asked. 'I have a plane to catch.'

Michelle laughed. 'And he likes to pretend not to hear what he doesn't want to hear.'

'So tell me about your unusual childhood,' said Sky, and smiled blithely at Chase, who smiled back blandly.

'Perhaps another time,' he said evenly.

Sky felt a little devil stir inside her. 'Maybe Michelle will tell me,' she said.

'I don't think so.' Chase's face was calm, but his voice held a hint of warning. 'Am I going to have that tea, or not?'

Michelle dutifully took the teapot and filled the cups. She handed one to Sky. There was a glint of humour in her dark eyes that did not escape Sky.

The mysteries of Chase's youth were not to be revealed. He had not wanted to hear the subject mentioned. There were altogether too many unknowns for her sense of comfort. Sky wondered if he'd want to hear about the subject of the Ecuador hotel. It was worth a try. She felt suddenly deliciously reckless. She tapped the magazine next to her on the sofa. 'I was leafing through this and my eye caught something about the Ecuador hotel. It appears that there are some problems because of its size.'

He nodded. 'Yes.' He seemed unconcerned.

'Was it a big disappointment?' she asked.

'No. I had predicted it.'

His calm reply threw her off-balance. It was not what she had expected.

'Then why did you go through with it?'

'Because my obstinate little brother needed an object-lesson. He wouldn't listen and I decided the only way he was going to see the light was to go ahead with the planning stage and let him see what would happen from experience.' He gave a crooked smile. 'He's getting his object-lesson.'

Sky stirred sugar into her tea and frowned. 'There's something I don't understand. At the party you wanted to know what I thought about the project and then when I did you told me to keep my opinion to myself. Why?'

His mouth quirked. 'That was only for your own good. Everybody in that room was interested in the big hotel and the big profits. They would not have appreciated your environmental concerns.' He lifted his cup to his mouth.

'I didn't think you did either!'

'Oh, I did, indeed, but I was taking Breck's place at that affair and I had to show some loyalty in public. My personal convictions were not relevant at that particular gathering.' He put his cup back on the table. 'Now, I think we need to finish up here.' He took out a map.

'I'll leave you to it,' said Michelle, and left the room.

Chase told her about the possibilities of the island, his finger moving over the map, and Sky took notes.

'When you take your pictures,' he instructed, 'I want you to concentrate on the sort of thing that would appeal to naturalists and sports people.'

She listened and scribbled, and downed two more cups of tea while wonderful visions swirled through her head. Yet all the while she was acutely aware of his nearness and the sound of his voice.

Later, as she was ready to leave, he saw her to the front door. She felt light with excitement, and he looked down at her face, his mouth curved in a smile.

'You're going to enjoy it,' he said.

Her heart thumped at the look in his eyes. 'Oh, I know I will!' It was impossible to keep her voice businesslike. She was simply too excited.

She wished he'd open the door, but he just stood there looking at her with those light green eyes that made her blood pump wildly through her. His hand reached out and lightly touched her cheek.

'I wish I were on the island with you tonight, right now. There's a special place by the beach, secluded and very... romantic.' He lowered his face to hers. 'I would kiss you... like this.' He cradled her face in his hands and kissed her, a soft, sensuous kiss that made her every cell quiver in response.

'And then I would hold you very close.' His voice had a soft, hypnotic quality and she yielded to him as he pressed her against him as if he did not want to let her go, as if he wanted her shape imprinted on his body. All her senses responded to the feel of his hard strength against her. Her blood sang. She stood in his embrace, mesmerised.

'And then,' he went on, his voice low and seductive, 'I would make passionate love to you, right there under the stars.'

Magic. Madness.

Gathering the shreds of her shattered control, she tried to pull free from his embrace. He let her go easily and she stepped back from him on trembling legs, fighting to regain some semblance of composure. The last thing she wanted was for him to see how much he affected her with that seductive voice, those erotic images.

'No doubt you're very good at seducing women,' she said, trying to sound light and casual, 'but I have no intention of letting you seduce me.'

His eyes glinted devilishly. 'But maybe you won't be able to resist,' he said softly.

She clenched her hands. 'Maybe I'm stronger and more determined than you think.' Her voice quivered nervously and she could hear it herself.

He gave a low laugh. 'Really? Well, in that case I'll read the *Wall Street Journal*.' He reached for the door and opened it for her with a flourish. 'And now I have a plane to catch.' His eyes had not left her face. 'Goodbye, Sky. I'll see you soon.'

It was a promise.

She climbed into her Jeep and leaned her head on the steering-wheel, taking in a deep breath.

She drove home on automatic, seeing his eyes, hearing his hypnotic voice, feeling and tasting his kiss, wondering what it would be like to make love with him under the stars.

Flying in a tiny puddle-jumper was a thrilling adventure. She felt surrounded by sky and sea, with nothing substantial to protect her from either. It was like flying in a car.

Sky shared this seemingly flimsy contraption with a herpetologist—a reptile and amphibian expert who was doing a study on rare and endemic species of lizards on tiny Caribbean islands.

He came from Florida and his name was Paul Santelli. He had dark hair, deep blue eyes and a contagious laugh. Since Sky was also interested in lizards, albeit for their photogenic qualities, they engaged in an animated discussion about geckos, iguanas and chameleons for the short duration of the flight.

Paul could not believe his luck in coming across a professional wildlife photographer, and asked if perhaps they could join forces for the sake of science and go in pursuit of reptiles together one day. He would be delighted to have some professional photographs and his expertise in locating and identifying the creatures could be of help to her. Recognising an opportunity when she saw one, Sky agreed happily.

The island was coming into view—forest-covered hills, palm-fringed white beaches, surrounded by placid, sun-shot waters below displaying an array of translucent blues and greens. It was more beautiful than any pictures she had ever seen and she felt a growing excitement.

Fifteen minutes later they were off the plane, through Customs and Passport Control and in Mum's Taxi, the only one on the island. The radio throbbed reggae music and the driver sang lustily along with the tune.

The small capital of Port Royal was a cheerful and slightly ramshackle collection of colourful buildings of various colonial styles. People were everywhere in the narrow streets, laughing, talking, selling fruit or roasted plantain. They stopped in front of a baby-blue building, the Sugar Bay hotel, where Paul got out. He gave her a wide grin and told her he'd call her after he'd found his bearings.

On they drove, out of the town, down the coastal road past picturesque little coves, coconut palm groves, and small villages with pastel-coloured houses—turquoise, sugar-pink, violet. Just outside the fishing village of Ginger Bay, the driver turned off the road on to a narrow unpaved track and the car lurched and shuddered up to a rustic cabin built into the hillside and surrounded by lush tropical foliage.

Sky stared at the modest place and frowned. Surely this was not Chase's island villa?

'I don't think this is it,' she said uncertainly. She held out the paper with the address for the driver to see. He laughed.

'Oh, yes, dis is de place, mahm. Doan worry.'

She climbed out of the car and walked up the short path on to a thatched terrace. The terrace was merely an open-air extension of the cabin, which had no front wall and no door. It was simply open,

cabana style. Anything and anybody could march
right in and walk away with the furniture . . . which,
she saw, was made of rugged rattan. The sofa and
chairs had thick cushions covered with bright island
fabric. She stood on the terrace, glancing around
apprehensively. Was she supposed to just walk in?
Well, what other choice did she have?

She walked in. There was no one there. What if
the driver was wrong and this was not Chase's
place? It would be very embarrassing to install
herself here and then have the owner or owners
come home to find her. She grinned to herself. She
could just imagine the scene.

Then her eyes caught a magazine on the coffee-
table and the now familiar logo of the Montana
Group. All right, OK, this then had to be Chase's
place. She turned and found the driver already un-
loading her gear on to the terrace.

'You're right, this is the place,' she said and the
man shook his head.

'I tell you dis is de place. Why you doan believe
a wise old man?'

Sky laughed. 'Because I'm dumb and young.' She
paid him and added a generous tip which he took
with a grin.

Back inside she glanced around the bright, cosy
room. The cabin had no ceiling and she looked
straight up into the thatch of the roof which was
made of some sort of natural material. A large
bookcase stacked full of books and magazines took
up space on one wall. Primitive paintings depicting
cheerful island scenes decorated the others. A rustic
woven mat lay on the smooth wooden floor. It was
a wonderful, airy place. Breezes from outside

wafted through the house. The whispering of the
palm fronds was audible everywhere, and from the
terrace a wide expanse of aquamarine sea was
visible. The ambience was one of romance and intimacy; it was a special place, a very private
sanctuary.

Chase's cabin. She bit her lip and closed her eyes.
The image of the fish on the line sprang into her
consciousness with vivid clarity. Not only had Chase
lured her to an idyllic little island, he had lured her
straight into his love nest ...

She explored the rest of the cottage, which took
little time. There were two bedrooms and one
bathroom. The kitchen was small, but had the
necessary equipment including a fridge stocked with
cold roast chicken and fruit salad. Mrs Drakes, apparently, had been alerted as to her arrival.

She didn't have to go far to find wildlife, Sky
realised. Lizards scurried in the thatch overhead, a
yellow banana quit hopped around on the terrace
table looking for food. Hummingbirds fluttered
frantically around the purple bougainvillaea
framing the terrace.

Over the next few days she explored the island
in the little white Mini Moke for which Chase had
given her the keys, the tradewind breezes wafting
sensuously through her hair. She went on a photographing orgy. The world was full of beauty and
surprises—bread fruit trees, almond trees, ginger
thomas trees with their yellow trumpet-shaped
flowers, green lizards and bright blue birds and
clouds of purple butterflies. She photographed
fishermen hauling in their nets, women peeling
nutmegs, farmers cutting enormous stalks of

bananas, and children playing with a pet pig. She felt drunk with excitement, ecstatic with delight. This speck of an island was paradise!

'I doan understand,' said Mrs Drakes, the house-keeper, looking at the heap of laundry at her feet in bewilderment. 'What you do alla time? Where you go?'

Sky waved her hand. 'Everywhere.' Her clothes were not a pretty sight. Grass and mud stains were everywhere. One of her shirts had a ripped sleeve. The first few days, Mrs Drakes had said nothing. Now, apparently, she thought it was time to investigate this abominable state of affairs.

Mrs Drakes was twice Sky's size. She had a round body clad in a neat, flowered dress, and a beautiful face with a warm smile. She lived in Ginger Bay and walked up the rocky track every morning to take care of the housework. She was shaking her head at Sky.

'I doan expect girl clothes to look like dis,' she said, sounding like a mother—not Sky's mother, but somebody else's, which she was, having three pretty daughters. Sky had seen the daughters on Sunday in front of the Ark of Love Catholic church. They'd worn frilly dresses, white socks, shiny black shoes and colourful clips and bows in their neatly plaited hair. They'd practically shone with cleanliness and good care.

'Mr Montana, yes, his clothes dey always like dis,' Mrs Drakes went on. '*Worse* dahn dis, but I know he wild and crazy, daht man, but you—a pretty girl like you——' She gave Sky a meaningful look and did not finish the sentence. There was no need to. Sky understood perfectly.

'I'm a wildlife photographer,' she explained. 'I lie or sit on the ground, I climb rocks and trees. I get dirty.'

Mrs Drakes was unimpressed and went on shaking her head. 'Look at you,' she said, pointing at Sky's legs. 'Where you get daht scratch, and daht bruise?'

'I fell,' said Sky. 'My foot slipped.'

'Where you go?'

'I went to the Rocks.' The Rocks indicated the rocky north-east coast on the Atlantic side of the island.

'People get killed dere! Last year, a crazy Englishmahn fell and broke his neck!'

'I'm very tough,' Sky said reassuringly. 'And in my whole life I've only broken two bones—an arm and a leg.'

From Mrs Drakes' shocked face it was apparent that she did not consider two broken bones a reassuring statistic. 'Mr Montana know you climb rocks and trees?' she asked suspiciously.

No, he didn't. He had, in fact, told her not to. 'He's paying me to take pictures of the island, Mrs Drakes,' Sky said evasively. 'You don't have to worry. It's my job. I'm a professional.' She glanced at the heap of laundry. 'And don't worry about the clothes. They're old. It doesn't matter if the stains don't all come out.'

The woman looked indignant. 'Of course dey'll come out! I'm only saying I tink some'ing is wrong.'

'Nothing is wrong,' Sky reassured her. 'I'm just wild and crazy, like Mr Montana.'

Her own words echoed in her head. She frowned.
Wild and crazy like Chase? Chase in his impeccable clothes was anything but wild and crazy.
However, Mrs Drakes seemed to have a different
opinion.

'What kind of things does Mr Montana do when
he's here?' she asked.

'He climb rocks,' said Mrs Drakes disapprov-
ingly. 'And he camp in the forest on the moun-
tains! It's dangerous!'

'Why is it dangerous?'

'Snakes, insects.' She paused. 'And spirits,' she
added in a whisper.

To Sky, snakes and insects were nothing new.
Spirits were. It sounded very intriguing. 'What kind
of spirits?' she asked.

But Mrs Drakes was suddenly very busy with the
laundry and missed the question. Well, that was
what it looked like.

'He wild and crazy, daht mahn.' The words seemed
to follow her as Sky hiked through the dim green
light of the mountain rainforest on her way back
to the campsite she'd found earlier that day. It was
a wonderful spot right by the side of a bubbling
stream that tumbled lustily down the mountain
across boulders and rocks.

She'd assumed Chase was more the tennis, golf
and yachting type of sportsman. It seemed to fit
the sleek image she had of him. Now Mrs Drakes
called him wild and crazy. She frowned. More and
more things didn't make sense. But then nothing
had made much sense since the very beginning.
Chase confused her. Among other things. She

moaned in frustration. It was as if he'd put a spell on her and she was doing and thinking and feeling things she shouldn't be. Carefully she stepped over a moss-covered tree-trunk that had fallen across the trail.

The last couple of days she had spent with Paul in search of lizards, and she'd got some wonderful shots. Many of them, she was sure, she would not have been able to make without Paul's help and expertise. His enthusiasm for the creatures was contagious and she'd come away knowing more about lizards than she'd ever thought she wanted to know. She grinned now as she scanned the trees around her, hoping, as she had hoped all day, to find a parrot, but not one showed itself.

Coming closer to the campsite, she smelled woodsmoke, and as she reached the clearing by the stream her heart leaped into her throat.

Chase was standing by the fire, feeding it small dead branches. The sleek businessman was gone. He was wearing khaki shorts, a T-shirt and sports shoes and his bare legs and arms were muscled and brown. Big and hard-muscled, he emanated a rugged male virility. He looked perfectly at home in this primitive green wilderness. Another backpack lay next to hers, a tent tied to the top of it.

Her heartbeat went wild. Excitement, trepidation. She was not ready to face this man. It was suddenly clear how much it took out of her to see him, how fragile her emotional state was, how few her defences.

He looked up when he heard her approach and across the short distance his gaze met hers. She took

in the dark glitter of his eyes and the hard line of
his jaw and a shiver of fear ran down her spine. In
spite of the sultry heat surrounding her, she felt
herself grow icy cold.

CHAPTER SIX

'I was just about to start looking for you,' Chase said without as much as a greeting. 'Didn't I tell you not to go into the forest by yourself?'

Yes, Daddy, she was tempted to say, but the look on his face prevented her from uttering the words. Here was a big, powerful man who was used to having his directions and orders followed, and she, a temporary minor underling, had chosen not to. In his khaki shorts and T-shirt he exuded an elemental, tough masculinity that was exciting and frightening at the same time. She bit her lip and said nothing.

He snapped a stick in two and tossed the pieces into the fire. 'I told you specifically *not* to go into the forest by yourself!' His voice was gritty with anger.

She shrugged lightly, feigning a cool composure she didn't feel. 'Did you? I don't remember,' she said casually, untangling herself from her camera equipment slung over her shoulders.

His jaw went rigid. 'You damn well remember! And I also told you not to go climbing the Rocks and I understand from Mrs Drakes that you've done just that!'

This was too much. He was not her keeper or her parole officer. She glared at him. 'I'm on my own all the time! I know what I'm doing! You gave me an assignment, now let me do it my way! I can't do it if I can't go where I'm supposed to go, can I?'

'You couldn't wait a few lousy days until I could take you?'

'You? Take me around? You said you had work to do here. I wasn't expecting you to trail me while I'm working.'

He glowered at her. 'I know where the good spots are, the right places. And I had most certainly planned to come with you into the rainforest and to the Rocks. It's not safe alone.'

Her body was tense with the effort to stay under control. 'I appreciate your concern, but I'm not a nitwit. I don't take stupid chances. I can't work with people hanging around. I need peace and quiet while I work. It takes concentration!'

'You can have all the peace and quiet you want,' he said, his face hard.

'Not with you around,' she snapped. 'You aggravate me.'

His eyes bored into hers. 'I don't think I aggravate you. At least not in the way you want me to think.'

Her heart beat erratically. He knew and sensed too much. He understood what she wasn't willing to admit even to herself.

'I want you to leave me alone!' she said fiercely. 'And you can start by picking up your pack and getting out of here right now!'

'I'm not leaving.' Grim, cold, determined.

'Well, then *I* am!'

'Oh, no, you're not. It's almost dark.'

'Watch me!' She didn't know what got into her. It was dangerous to go tramping through the forest at night. She knew that. It was stupid even to suggest it, yet some crazy force had taken over her mind. She bent over and yanked one of the tent spikes out of the ground. Chase grabbed her wrist.

'Stop it! Don't be an idiot!'

She grew rigid. 'Are you going to keep me here against my will?'

'If I have to.'

'And how do you propose to do that?'

Something glinted in his green eyes. He shrugged casually. 'I could tie you up.'

She wouldn't put it past him. 'A cave man, are you? How civilised.' She tried to wrench her wrist free, to no avail. His hand was like a vice. Fury rushed through her like fire.

'I hate you!' she whispered fiercely.

'Oh, no, you don't,' he said calmly, and released her hand. 'I think, Sky, that you have feelings for me you don't want to admit to. You want me, and you're fighting it.'

The arrogance of the man! The audacity! 'I don't want you!' She was practically shouting, and a couple of birds near by flew off in a flurry of fear. Something snapped inside her. 'I don't like who you are and what you do!' She was shaking and in the far recesses of her mind she knew she had lost it, that her tongue was again sprinting ahead of her reason.

A tense silence shivered between them as his eyes held hers. Even the birds seemed to be quiet.

'Well, that's a first,' he said coldly, 'I must admit. I don't recall anyone ever saying that to my face.' He paused while he studied her. 'So tell me,' he said then, his voice deceptively casual, 'who am I and what is it that I do that bothers you so?'

'You're too damned arrogant! You manipulate people! You think you can have whatever you want! You cut down rainforests! You bring hordes of tourists where they have no business being! And all of that for *money*, for profit!'

His eyes were a hard green glitter. 'I haven't cut down a single damned inch of rainforest anywhere,' he bit out. 'You might have acquainted yourself with some pertinent facts before you made accusations.'

'So you're planning to! Or at least your company is! What would you call that hotel in Ecuador? A motel on the New Jersey turnpike?'

'That hotel was never going to happen,' he said coldly. 'I told you that.'

'And what about all those other hotels?'

He gave her a chilling look. 'They're located on the French Riviera, the Costa Brava in Spain, in Hong Kong, Singapore, Rio de Janeiro, New York, California and places like that.' He paused significantly. 'Not exactly virgin tourist territory, wouldn't you say?'

Not exactly. Sky did not enjoy feeling stupid and she was not having a good time digesting this information. She'd made accusations and assumptions not even knowing the most basic facts. It was humiliating.

'No.' She felt swamped with guilt. She stared into the fire, feeling like a fool, hating herself for talking in anger and losing control over her brain. Gathering whatever was left of her dignity, she met his eyes. 'I'm sorry,' she said awkwardly. 'I talk too much and I don't think enough. I was out of line.'

'Well, maybe it's just as well you got your suspicions off your mind.' He strode off and picked up a dead branch a little way down the track, effectively terminating the conversation.

She felt drained, a feeling that had nothing to do with her physical fatigue, which was also coming into play. She dug into her backpack and took out her toiletry bag, a towel and clean clothes. She walked off, following the stream to a secluded spot, and stripped off her clothes to have a bath.

The water was frigid, and it chilled her body as well as her emotions and gave her an opportunity to think clearly. His sudden appearance at her camp had left her unprepared. She'd been over-reacting and her anger had been a cover-up for her fear.

She was afraid of Chase. She was afraid of herself, afraid of her own feelings, of the way she responded to him, in some primitive, natural sort of way she had no control over. Shivering, she dried quickly and put on loose cotton trousers and a T-shirt. She'd have to keep her head cool, which was no problem at this very moment because all of her was more than cool. She shivered again, then made her way back to the fire, taking a deep, fortifying breath as she saw Chase come into view.

He'd set up his little tent not far from hers and a blackened pot was sitting in the hot coals. He was sitting comfortably against a tree-trunk, drinking from a green enamel mug. 'Care for some wine?' he asked, holding up a bottle. His voice was calm, his manner casual. Let's forget what happened, said his attitude.

The storm had blown over and she'd take her cue from him.

'Yes, please,' she said evenly. She handed him the enamel mug from her backpack, then extracted a small pan, intending to fill it with water from the stream and cook herself a meal.

'Dinner's on me,' he said, guessing her intention. 'That is, if you like Mrs Drakes' rice and curried goat. She had some frozen in the freezer.'

'I do, thanks. She cooked it for me a few days ago. It's good.' It certainly was better than the tasteless freeze-dried chicken something she had in a little packet in her pack. She sat down, her back against a tree-trunk. It felt good to get off her feet. Taking a drink of her wine, she watched a small blue and white bird perched on a branch near by, singing lustily.

'How did you do today?' he asked.

'Great. This place is wonderful.' It seemed a strain to conduct a normal conversation. She felt small and stupid and regretted her accusations.

'See any parrots?'

She shook her head. 'No. I looked myself silly.'

'They're not easy to find.' He got to his feet and gathered towel and clothes. 'I'll be back soon. Stir the goat once or twice, will you?'

After he came back from his ablutions, they ate the tasty, spicy food. Goat was a common meat on the island, Mrs Drakes had told her. It made her think of something Chase had said to her weeks ago.

'You once told me you learned to kill chickens and butcher goats on some sort of farm,' she said. 'What kind of farm was that?'

'A survival camp.' There was a sardonic twist to his mouth.

'A survival camp?'

'Yes. Or, more correctly, a juvenile correctional facility.' He spooned more rice and curry into his mouth.

The surprise was so big that for a moment she could not digest the meaning.

'A juvenile correctional facility?' she echoed. 'What were you doing there?'

'I was being corrected,' he said drily.

She stared at him, incredulous. The spoon slipped out of her fingers on to the ground. 'Are you telling me you were a...a...?' The idea was so preposterous that she had trouble getting the words out. 'Were you a juvenile delinquent?'

The phrase juvenile delinquent conjured images of teenagers holding up petrol-station attendants, selling drugs to their friends, or mugging little old ladies. Although she did not have any illusion about Chase possessing a pure and pristine soul, she could not imagine him doing anything as villainous as mugging a little old grandma.

'I was on the way to becoming one.' He gave a lop-sided grin. 'My dear daddy put me in the camp voluntarily to avoid my ending up in gaol. I was headed there, in his opinion, and he intended to take matters in hand before the police or some other authority would deem it necessary to take charge of me. My father liked to be firmly in control of family matters.'

'I see.' She wasn't sure that she did. She'd never met a man who'd learned how to butcher a goat in a juvenile correctional facility. It did not sound at

all promising; he didn't sound at all like the sort
of man your parents would want you to bring home
for Sunday dinner.

'Best thing that ever happened to me,' Chase said
casually. 'Slapped me right into shape.'

'What did you do that was so terrible?'

'I was out of control. I stayed out at night and
didn't want anybody telling me how to live my life.
Then one day I—er—borrowed my mother's car
before I had a driver's licence, swiped one of her
credit cards, and took off for Virginia Beach for a
week and hung out with a bunch of college students
on spring break. I drank and smoked and partied
and crashed my mother's car into a parking-lot
lamp-post.'

She stared at him. 'What was *wrong* with you?'

He gave a crooked grin. 'I suffered from an easy
life. No challenges, lots of money, no goals. I was
bored and looked for stimulation in all the wrong
places.'

She could just imagine. 'And now you're no
longer bored,' she concluded.

'Haven't been bored since they told me to fish
and hunt for my own food and cook it on my own
fire, or starve.'

'I can see how that could motivate you into
action.'

'They had some innovative techniques,' he commented. 'And they certainly worked for me.'

She tilted her head and considered him. 'And here
you are, a hotel tycoon. Your daddy must have been
proud.'

'He never expected anything else, survival camp
or not.' He put down his empty plate.

She retrieved her spoon from the ground and wiped it with her paper napkin. 'I suppose when Michelle made a reference to your unusual teenage years this camp was what she was talking about.'

'Yes.'

'How long were you there? When did you get out?'

'I was there for a couple of years. I got out when I was seventeen and was accepted at Harvard.'

'*Harvard*?'

'Nobody ever said I was stupid,' he said wryly, 'just wild and crazy.'

These had been Mrs Drakes' words, too. '*I know he wild and crazy, daht mahn.*' Sky stared silently into the fire. This was quite some food for thought. She felt as if she'd been thrown into a maelstrom of images and words and ideas, and suddenly nothing made sense any more, not who Chase was, not her own opinions of him and his life, nothing. It was a scary feeling, as if suddenly she had nothing to hold on to and she was tossed around by an uncontrollable force.

He poured a little more wine into her mug, giving her a crooked smile. 'You look confused,' he commented. 'Have another drink.'

She wasn't sure that more wine was what she needed, but she accepted it without a word and sipped it slowly. She finished her food in silence, trying to make sense out of all the odd bits and pieces that made up the character of the man sitting beside her. Darkness was falling fast and she picked up the dishes and went to wash them by the stream.

He was making coffee when she came back. It was still early, but it seemed as if deep night surrounded them. The piercing shrieks of cicadas and other insects throbbed in the air. The tree canopy hid the sky and not a star was visible above.

'What kind of nature resort are you thinking of building here?' she asked as she took the mug of coffee he handed her.

Some years ago, he said, he had decided that the Montana Group needed to branch out into a different sort of tourism. He wanted to establish small, exclusive nature resorts in the more remote and exciting places of the world, the places that would attract the adventurous wealthy tired of the standard thing. They would pay a premium price to see and experience the real, unspoiled thing—in the rough. No luxury.

'Local governments are becoming more and more aware of how valuable their natural resources are and that they need to be managed carefully and——'

'I know,' Sky said. 'What they need is money to protect them against poachers and slash-and-burn farming and lumber companies and destructive mass tourism.' Mass tourism tended to change the character or even destroy the very thing the people came to admire, which was a loss for everyone.

'Right.' He put another log on the fire. The smoke held the insects at a distance. A tree frog gave a high-pitched shriek in a tree near by.

St Barlow, because of its size and variety of natural beauty, was ideal for a small nature camp. A few simple cottages could be built; tents would be used in the forest. It was a marvellous place for hikers, rock-climbers, scuba-divers and fishermen. The island government could levy a stiff fee for the use of their island and the revenue could support the economy and the protection of the environment.

They finished the wine as they talked by the glow of the fire, listening to the mysterious rustles and stirrings all around in the trees and on the leafy forest floor. Although it was still early, Sky felt fatigue overwhelm her. Her whole body began to droop as if her bones could no longer hold her up. She wished Chase goodnight and crawled into her tent, practically dragging herself. She fell asleep almost immediately, the maniacal screeching of the insects notwithstanding.

Bird song awoke her early the next morning. Zipping open her tent, she found pale light filtering through the canopy. Chase was already up and a pot of water bubbled on the fire.

'Good morning,' he said. 'Coffee?'

'Oh, please. I'll be right out.'

They had breakfast of wild guavas, sweet coconut bread and coffee. He asked her what her plans were for the day and she said she wanted to explore the forest more. He took her higher up the mountain into the cloud forest where the air was thickly humid and the vegetation wilder and more verdant with huge ferns, delicate orchids and lianas the size of thick ropes drooping down from the trees. The path was muddy and slippery and dead tree logs were covered with colourful lichen and fungi. It was a naturalist's paradise and Sky shot several rolls of film, feeling a sense of wonder overwhelming everything else as she worked—everything except the awareness of Chase by her side.

*   *   *

If Sky had expected a seduction campaign from
Chase, she was proved wrong. Chase was all polite
courtesy and helpfulness in the following days. He
did not touch her or make any sort of sexual ad-
vances, yet in spite of this the atmosphere between
them was heavy with tension and undercurrents.
Living with him in the close confines of the small
cabin was difficult and Sky couldn't look at him
without feeling her stomach twist with anxiety.

He'd borrowed a Mini Moke for his own use from
a friend who was not presently on the island. He
spent some time in Port Royal doing business, but
most of the time he was with her, showing her the
sights she had not seen before. He knew the island
as if he had lived there all his life and it was clear
that he'd done some serious exploring. He knew
hidden coves and secret places and spectacular
panoramas and waterfalls. He was in his element
here, she realised. As she saw so much of him every
day, living together in the small cabin, it became
increasingly clear to Sky that she didn't know Chase
very well.

She also realised that the business matters he
needed to take care of didn't require several weeks.

'You seem to have taken out a lot of time to do
very little business,' she said casually one day. They
were sitting on a dead log in the forest, taking a
break.

'I couldn't very well let you run loose on the
island by yourself. You might have gotten lost.'

'I can see how that's a great concern. So many
endless miles of road, such vast open spaces.'

'I wanted to get to know you,' he said then. 'I
wanted to spend time with you.' His voice was even.

She studied his face, allowing a short but significant pause. 'So you tempted me, trapped me, and now you're keeping me captive in paradise.'

One corner of his mouth twitched. 'Keep you captive? Is that how you feel—captive?'

She gave a wry smile. 'I allowed it to happen. I wanted the job.'

He met her eyes. 'Was that the only reason?'

It was hard to breathe. She tore her gaze away and stared into the lush green foliage.

He took her hand. It was the first time he had touched her in the five days he'd been on the island and the sensation was like an electric charge. She sat very still, willing her heart to calm down.

'I know I have no right to ask you this, but I will anyway. I'm asking you to trust me.'

He knew she didn't. Yet she wished with a sudden aching hunger that she did. That she could trust him. That she could trust her own feelings.

'Look at me, Sky.'

She swallowed hard and met his eyes.

'Don't be afraid,' he said softly.

She closed her eyes briefly. 'It always goes wrong,' she heard herself say in a low voice.

'Why?'

'I want too much. I expect too much.'

Once she'd had it all—love, commitment, respect. It was what she wanted again, but maybe it was too much to ask.

He was silent for a moment. 'You want a man to love you.'

'Yes.'

'And you want him to respect your work.'

'Yes.' She looked away, focusing on a small crimson bird sitting near by singing its heart out.

'You want to share your hopes and dreams.'

'Yes.' At one time or another she had told him all these things and he had remembered them. His hand, strong and warm, was still holding hers. She wished her heart would calm down.

'Anything else?'

She smiled. 'Yes. I want to love the man who loves me, and respect his work.'

He grinned crookedly. 'Fair enough. Is that it?'

She nodded.

'I don't think that's wanting too much.'

'It seems to be. Maybe I had it too easy with Josh. Looking back, it all seemed so simple and uncomplicated.' She let her hand slip from his grasp. Picking up a twig, she poked around in the leafy forest ground. Small insects scuttled away for cover.

His big hand came down on hers to still the movement. 'Shh. Over there—look!'

She looked in the direction he indicated and her heart leaped with delight. A parrot with brilliant plumage sat on an overhanging branch. Orange, emerald-green, black. Her first parrot in the wild. Excitement soared and she reached for her camera automatically, her eyes not leaving the beautiful bird.

'That's the one,' said Chase in a low voice. 'They're nowhere else besides here on St Barlow.'

She managed to get several shots of the bird before it flew away into the woods. She sat back again on the log and grinned with delight and satisfaction, and he smiled back at her.

'One dream come true,' he commented, 'although in the scheme of things I suppose it's a minor one.'

She laughed. 'I'll take what I can get.'

His eyes held hers captive and her words hung in the air between them.

'Will you?' he asked softly.

She lowered her gaze, her heart suddenly racing, and again it was there, that unbearable ache twisting inside her, the need, the yearning. The camera slipped off her knees on to the damp, leafy ground.

'Oh, damn,' she muttered and picked it up, wiping it off.

Chase came to his feet. 'Let's go,' he said brusquely.

In spite of the growing tension between them it was a time of pure pleasure. Chase did not get impatient when she wanted to stop and take photos, no matter how long it took for her to get the right angle, the right light. Sometimes she'd get so involved she'd forget he was there and when she looked up there he would be—sitting on a rock, or in the sand, or on a tree stump, watching her.

'This must be so boring for you,' she said one day as they were sitting on the beach in a rocky cove.

He shook his head. 'No. I like watching you.' Her pulse quickened. He'd spoken with the even tone of simple truth. With her eyes on her camera in her lap, she busied herself rewinding the film and taking it out, popping in a new one at once.

'Does that make you uncomfortable?' he asked.

She put the camera down. 'I'm not sure,' she answered, brushing sand off her legs.

'Come here,' he said huskily. He drew her to him and she sat on her knees between his and he cradled her face between his hands and kissed her.

His mouth was warm and giving. His lips stroked hers, his tongue teasing the corners of her mouth— a kiss like music, like a delicate, elegant dance. He kissed her as if she were the most precious, beautiful thing in the world. She felt as if they were afloat in warm water.

A hunger sprang up and flooded her. A soft moan escaped her and his kiss deepened. His hands moved from her face to her neck and shoulders, down her bare arms, shifting to her hips. His mouth trailed down her neck, leaving a damp trail, down until his lips rested on the top of her breasts just above the fabric of her V-necked, sleeveless top. He grew very still, his body hard and tense. She put her hands on the back of his head, curling her fingers through his hair, holding him to her.

She felt the warmth and pressure of his face against her breasts, feeling weak with longing. He groaned, encircling her with his arms and rolling both of them over into the sand. They were lying on their sides and he was pressing her into him, holding her so tight, she could barely breathe. She wanted him with a fierce, mindless passion that blinded everything. She moulded herself against him, giving up all restraint, her mouth searching for his breathlessly.

The sun was warm on her skin and the sensuous lapping of the water was like erotic music drifting through her senses.

Then suddenly he released her, came to his feet and walked off, leaving her trembling in the sand.

'Chase?' It was nothing but a breathy whisper and no answer came. She curled up, taking in ragged breaths of air. Then slowly she sat up, her body moving with difficulty, and saw Chase out in the sea, his arms butterflying through the water in powerful strokes.

'Damn you,' she muttered, feeling tears flood her eyes, but there wasn't anything to blame him for, really. It was inevitable that this sort of thing should happen and she should be grateful he hadn't just gone ahead and ravished her right then and there, oblivious to responsibility and consequences. Certainly she had not been in much of a state of mind herself to think rationally. They'd come dangerously close to the flashpoint. It was a frightening thought and something that needed some serious consideration.

She watched him wade out of the shallows, his shorts dripping water. When he reached her she wordlessly handed him his T-shirt, a gesture more than simple courtesy.

He met her eyes. 'Thanks,' he said quietly. He dried off his face and hair with the shirt.

She gathered up her equipment and they drove home in silence. During dinner their conversation was casual and low-key, but the underlying vibrations were hard to deny. Afterwards he said he had to go into Port Royal to meet someone and left. She spent the evening alone, feeling restless. She went to bed early and listened to the peaceful whispering of the palm fronds outside her window.

Inside her there was no such serenity.

*　　*　　*

The next day he took her to the other side of the island to inspect the shallow tidal pools and explore the sea caves. Before them lay a rugged landscape that held a wild, primal beauty. The sea here was rougher than on the western coast, and waves broke and foamed up against the detached masses of rock. It was low tide and they explored the caves carved out of the rocks by the force of the sea. The shallows were alive with a variety of creatures—vivid-coloured sea anemones, baby eels, reef fish, hermit crabs, urchins. She was enthralled with the beauty of it all, amazed by Chase's knowledge.

'You know so much,' she said, sitting back, stretching her legs, which were cramping from her awkward positions.

He likes this, came the sudden thought. It was a light-headed, joyous sensation to realise that he shared her sense of wonder and excitement, that he was here with her because that was where he wanted to be. He wanted to look at rocky tidal pools with her, to marvel at the diversity of life, to climb rocks and enjoy the beauty of the scenery. She felt a warm glow spread through her.

The first time she'd met him he'd been an imposing, ruthless businessman in an immaculate dark suit, a man talking about investments and profits and destroying rainforest.

The man she was watching now was wearing muddy khaki shorts and a red T-shirt and was enjoying the rugged outdoors, a man determined to create possibilities for responsible eco-tourism. A man who enjoyed watching her work and found magic in her pictures.

She should have known it long ago, but she'd been blinded by suspicion, wrong assumptions and bad perceptions. Blinded, too, by her own fear. She watched him now as he sat on his haunches, studying something crawling around at the water's edge, his eyes intent.

What was wrong with this man?

Nothing. Nothing was wrong with this man. Everything was supremely right and she'd been too obtuse to see it. A wave of emotion washed over her—pure and clear and magic.

I love him, she thought, and her head was suddenly filled with a dizzying sensation of joy. She wanted to just sit there, feast her eyes on him and revel in this glorious new discovery, hug it to her like a prized possession.

He glanced up at her suddenly as if he'd sensed her watching him, as if he knew her thoughts. 'What are you smiling about?' he asked, looking amused.

'I'm just having a good time,' she said brightly, amazed at her quick, light-hearted reply. Not that it wasn't true—it was eminently true: she was having the time of her life. She pointed higher up the rocks. 'Are we going to climb up there? Can we get there?'

They could, but it was not your average hike in the country. By the time they'd found a good place to sit, on a smooth, narrow ledge, she was quite out of breath. The panorama was spectacular—a blue-green sea wild with large rocky outcroppings and foam spewing up high as the waves broke over them. It was quite a difference from the tranquil, crystalline Caribbean waters on the other side of the island and the soft white sand beaches.

The breeze cooled her heated face and she leaned
gratefully against the warm rock wall behind her.
Chase unpacked his backpack and they ate a
leisurely lunch of cold coconut chicken, bread rolls
and sliced mango that Mrs Drakes had packed for
them. The sun on her face was making her drowsy
and she wished she could stretch out and go to sleep
for just a little while. There was no room, and one
unguarded movement and she'd tumble right down
the craggy cliffs, which would not be a pleasant
experience.

'Don't go to sleep,' Chase warned. He took her
hand and held it. His warmth flowed over into her,
making her heart glow and her heart sing. They
just sat there, looking out over the sea, holding
hands like teenagers, while her body began to grow
warmer and warmer. Birds swooped overhead. The
sea roared. After what seemed like a breathless
eternity, he simply put his other hand behind her
head, drew her face close to his and kissed her.

The heat of his mouth ignited a fire inside her.
There was nothing tentative about his kiss, nothing
tentative about the message. His mouth was firm
and possessive and his kiss full of need. She kissed
him back without restraint, needing him, wanting
him, not caring now that he should know.

His fingers trailed through her hair, brushed
down her throat with tantalising little touches,
coming to rest at the top button of her shirt.

'Let me look at you,' he said against her lips.
His breath was warm. 'Let me touch you.' It was
like a foggy dream and she could not feel her bones,
as if she had melted against the rock.

He pushed the shirt open as his mouth made a damp trail along her throat down to the top of her breasts. He withdrew and leaned back against the rock, meeting her eyes, then lowering his gaze slowly to her breasts. She felt them strain against the flimsy lace of her bra, and her breath came in shallow little puffs. He unfastened the front clasp and her breasts came free, the sun touching her bare skin with sensual warmth.

For a moment Chase did not move, then he cupped one breast in his large hand and gently stroked the nipple with his thumb and an exquisite, tingling sensation spread instantly through her.

'You're beautiful,' he said, and bent his mouth to her breast, his lips and tongue doing delicate erotic things, and she forgot to breathe. Pressing herself against the sun-warmed rock behind her, she felt desire curling around inside her. She sucked in a desperate breath, her body trembling.

He drew away and leaned back, closing his eyes. He drew in a ragged breath. 'Oh, God,' he muttered, 'this is insanity.'

She took in the taut lines of his face and he opened his eyes, looking at her with a hungry yearning that shook her to the core.

'I want to make love,' he said huskily.

'We can't,' she whispered.

He drew in another deep breath. 'I know.' He looked meaningfully at the ledge, then gave her a slow smile. 'Even if I'd been smart enough to be prepared for this eventuality, this particular location does not lend itself to romantic gropings and grapplings.'

She laughed nervously, happy for the release of tension his choice of words provided. No doubt it had been on purpose. She closed her bra and buttoned her shirt with trembling hands.

'But there is tonight,' he said then, meeting her eyes. There was a question in the green depths, a question he needed answering.

'Yes,' she whispered, knowing it was the only answer.

He smiled and squeezed her hand, then glanced down the mass of rock they'd climbed, and would have to descend again.

'I think we'd better have another cup of coffee before we attempt to climb down.'

She sat through dinner in a haze. There were candles and wine. And after Mrs Drakes left they sat on the thatch-roof terrace with coffee and talked while tree frogs offered their high-pitched calls and insects performed their nightly concert. The air was fragrant with night-blooming jasmine and a full moon washed the sea in a silvery sheen. It was a night for romance, a night for love.

He came to his feet and took her hand, helping her up. He drew her against him, his mouth by her ear.

'Let me make love to you,' he said quietly. 'Let me make you happy.'

CHAPTER SEVEN

THE bed in Chase's room was big and awash with moonlight. He held Sky in his arms and kissed her deeply and she responded with an eagerness that made her weak-kneed and dizzy-headed. His hands travelled along her back and hips, moulding her to him and the feel of his heated, urgent body sent her blood rushing wildly through her.

'I want you,' he whispered against her lips. 'I want you in my arms, in my bed.'

His breath was warm on her mouth and his words slipped into her heart like warm wine. She let out an inarticulate little sound, half-moan, half-whisper. He trailed the damp tip of his tongue along her lips with erotic delicacy.

'I want to feel you naked against me and touch you and kiss you all over,' he went on. 'It's what I've wanted for a long time.'

'You've been such a gentleman,' she whispered on a breathless little laugh. It was hard to stand on her shaky legs. It was hard to breathe.

He leaned away a little to look at her face. 'I was going to do it right,' he said, smiling faintly. 'I wasn't taking any chances, but you didn't make it easy.' His hands slipped under her shirt, sliding over her back and around to the front, and cupped her breasts. 'You didn't want to be seduced, so I wasn't going to, but you practically drove me to insanity. And then this afternoon on the rocks...' He

groaned and closed his eyes. Then he took her shirt
and peeled it off over her head and tossed it on to
a chair. He bent his head and put his mouth in the
hollow between her breasts.

She was breathing raggedly, her body aflame with
need. She tangled her fingers in the warm thickness
of his hair, then trailed them down his neck. Her
body sang with frenzied desire. Outside the rush of
the wind stirring the palm fronds mingled with her
breathing. The sweet perfume of jasmine wafting
in through the window mingled with the scent of
him, an intoxicating mixture of romance and
passion.

He unfastened her bra and kissed her breasts, his
tongue teasing her nipples, the sensation a sweet,
aching torment. He took off the rest of her clothes
with deliberate slowness, kissing her breasts, her
stomach, her thighs. When she stood naked before
him, he ripped off his own clothes in sudden fierce
haste. Her heart leaped into her throat at the naked
beauty of his aroused body, the strong male lines
and shapes and textures.

She reached out to him and his skin was hot
under her hands as she let them slide across his chest
and stomach. He drew her to him with a groan and
her cheek against his hard chest registered the
thumping of his heart, beating a rhythm in harmony
with her own.

He lifted her up into his arms and eased her on
to the bed, lying down next to her. Love welled in
her heart as she saw his face lit by the moon, and
she reached up and rested her hand on his cheek.
She smiled into his eyes.

'I want you so much,' she whispered.

A tremor went through him and with a soft groan his mouth came down on hers in a fierce and passionate kiss.

She wrapped herself around him, pressing herself against him, wanting to feel every inch of him, her body feverish with the need to express her feelings. She kissed his mouth, his eyes, her hands roaming over his body, drinking in the feel of him. He groaned, kissing her back, then took her hands and gently untangled her from him.

'Not so fast,' he muttered thickly. 'My control has its limits.'

'I would hope so,' she murmured, feeling drunk with desire.

'And you've gone way past yours,' he whispered in her ear as he lowered himself against her.

'Don't embarrass me.' She squirmed beneath him and he laughed softly.

'I like it. I like honest passion in a woman.'

And then there were no more words, only sweet murmured sounds and whisperings as they breathlessly pleasured each other, their lovemaking more eloquent than words. She loved the way he touched her, his generous attention and unselfish giving. She answered his passion with all the love she felt for him until the throbbing, pulsing need of their bodies swept them into a swirling vortex of ecstasy. She clung to him mindlessly, helplessly, and all was sweet oblivion.

It seemed an eternity before her heart had resumed a normal rhythm and she could speak again, and then only to whisper his name against the warmth of his neck.

'Yes?' he said softly.

'You made me feel so wonderful,' she said.

'That was the whole idea, wasn't it?' He seemed amused. He cradled her warm and snug against his body, showing no intention of letting her go.

'Yes. But this was a special kind of wonderful,' she said, revelling in the delicious, lazy afterglow of lovemaking.

'As opposed to the run-of-the-mill variety of wonderful?'

She chuckled. 'Yes.'

'Well, let me tell you a secret.' He nuzzled her earlobe. 'It takes two to make it a special kind of wonderful.'

What it takes is love, she thought dimly, and she let the thought curl through her mind until sleep captured her tired, sated body.

In the morning she awoke to the feeling of his hands stroking her body. It was an exquisite way to wake up, feeling aroused and only semi-conscious. She let out a slow, delicious sigh, relishing his hands doing wonderfully erotic things to her while she lay there in drowsy immobility.

But eventually the drowsiness was stroked and kissed into oblivion and passion swept her away into paradise once more.

They lay in a tangle of sheets, legs entwined, breathing hard. 'You are quite a woman, Sky Malone,' he whispered breathlessly. 'I warn you now, I'm never going to get enough of you.'

'I was nineteen and I thought my life was over,' Sky said. 'I lost twelve pounds and couldn't work or study or concentrate or anything. I couldn't sleep. I lost a whole semester in college. My pictures were horrible, morbid, ugly things. I never wanted to photograph anything again. I wanted to die.'

Sky and Chase were at the beach for an afternoon swim and he had asked her to tell him about Josh. She would not, on her own, have initiated such a conversation, but he seemed genuinely interested in her and her life. Other men had not always been comfortable with the subject of her husband and marriage, but Chase seemed neither threatened nor disturbed by the fact that she had once loved another man. It was a relief and a joy to be with a man who was secure in himself.

Wet and refreshed from their swim, they were sitting in the shade of a coconut palm, having the tiny cove all to themselves. As she talked she looked out over the smooth sea, feeling the soft breeze touch her skin, and it was difficult to think back again to those dark, unhappy days while all around her the world was beautiful and serene.

She took a handful of sand and let it flow through her fingers. 'I was a mess and everybody was worried about me and I just didn't care about anything any more. Then one day Rocky came home and he packed me up and took me to Oregon and with a couple of his friends we went white-water rafting down the Rogue river. It was the most terrifying adventure I ever lived through and all I did was scream at Rocky like a madwoman and call him every vile name known to man and he just pretended not to hear me.'

She smiled suddenly. 'It made me realise I wasn't ready to die. Also, it took so much energy out of me that I had little time to wallow in my grief, which was exactly why Rocky had taken me. I didn't know until later than he'd organised the expedition just for me, and for that purpose. He'd known that the only thing that could get my mind off my misery was a big helping of primal, heart-stopping fear.'

Chase lay on his back in the sand, looking up at the azure sky, squinting against the bright light. 'You love him, don't you?'

'Of course I do. He's the best brother anybody could ever have. He's there when you need him. When things get really tough, you can count on him.'

There was a silence, until suddenly, in one swift movement, Chase turned over, pushed her down on to her back in the sand, rolled on top of her and kissed her hard.

The sudden passion of his kiss overwhelmed her and when finally he lifted his head she laughed breathlessly. 'Wow,' she said, 'you wild and crazy, mahn.'

His eyes were oddly dark and he didn't smile.

A treacherous uneasiness stirred around inside her. She pushed it back. She loved this man and life was wonderful.

If only she wouldn't wake up one morning and find that it had all been a dream.

They went scuba-diving the next day. Floating free and weightless in the water was one of the most exquisite feelings Sky knew and the magical under-water world of fish, plants and coral gardens was a treasure of colour and shape and movement. Fish in rainbow colours swam by, iridescent blue, yellow, orange and purple.

It was the first opportunity she'd had to go diving since Rocky had taught her the basics in Florida years ago. She had enjoyed it immensely then, but the high cost of travel and equipment made it too expensive a sport for her to pursue.

Now here she was with Chase, sharing with him the wondrous beauty of marine life, and elation filled her at the thought of exploring with him new places, new worlds. Thinking of the future brought secret thrills of excitement.

That night they perused a stack of maps and travel books and made a list of magical places in the world crying out for rustic nature camps, places begging to be documented in her photo book— exotic islands, rainforests in remote areas, hidden mountain villages, wild rivers, mysterious deserts.

'Where do you want to go first?' he asked.

It took no time to think. 'Africa! I'd love to go to Africa!'

Chase studied her face, a faint smile curving his mouth. He trailed his index finger slowly around the contours of her mouth. 'Do you know what we're doing?' he asked softly.

'Yes,' she whispered. She knew exactly what they were doing.

They were dreaming and planning together.

They were golden days, and it was a little frightening to be so happy, but she pushed the pin-pricks of fear away and laughed and smiled through the days. The weather was perfect, the food was perfect, her job was perfect, and Chase was perfect.

One evening while Chase was out wining and dining the ministers of finance, commerce, and industry, Sky was alone in the cottage when her mother called.

She asked how Sky was doing, and Sky told her she couldn't possibly be doing better and the island was absolute paradise and the job was wonderful and the weather was glorious. She stopped there. She couldn't quite bring herself to tell her mother that her nights were magical and full of passion, spent in the arms of the man she loved.

'You sound very happy,' her mother said drily.

Sky had no doubt that her mother knew exactly what she wasn't being told. She grinned into the mouthpiece. 'I feel very happy,' she acknowledged. 'Have you heard from Rocky yet?'

'He came home two days ago.' The tone of her mother's voice seemed a bit off, not quite as enthusiastic as Sky had expected it to sound.

'What about his girlfriend?' she asked. 'Did he bring her?'

'Yes, yes, he did.'

'Tell me about her. Do you like her?' It was quite possible that her mother was not ecstatic about the girl. She might have purple hair, a ring through her nose, or belong to an exotic cult. You could never quite tell what Rocky would acquire on his trips across the world's oceans and some things were even too far out for her tolerant, easygoing mother.

'Oh, she's very nice!' said her mother, sounding as if she meant it. 'She's quiet, and she seems very...smart.'

This did not sound like the sort of girl who gravitated towards Rocky. 'I thought Rocky liked the outgoing, gushy type. How old is she? What does she look like?'

'She's twenty-nine and she's dark-haired and pretty in a quiet sort of way.'

Sky listened with amazement. Rocky was thirty and he'd always gone for the perky young things who looked up to him in awe and thought he was a blond god from the sea. 'Oh, my, a mature woman, Mom. What happened to Rocky?'

'Maybe he's growing up,' said her mother wryly. 'He did turn thirty this year. Not that I noticed, though.' She took a deep breath. 'Sky, I need to talk to you.' Her voice suddenly took on a desperate note.

'What's wrong?'

'Oh, Sky!' she wailed. 'I don't know how to tell you!'

'I don't know either,' said Sky, not knowing what her mother was referring to. 'Is Dad all right?'

'Oh, yes, fine, fine.' Another desperate gulp of air. 'Do you remember the time, years ago, when Rocky was in the Caribbean for a couple of years? When he started that scuba-diving business?'

Sky frowned, trying to remember. 'Vaguely.' Keeping track of Rocky's ventures and wanderings in various places was not an easy proposition. 'What about it?'

'He was working with a . . . a partner; do you remember that? And they were doing very well.' She heard her mother draw in a deep breath. 'His partner wanted to expand the business into a more up-scale affair and Rocky didn't want to. Remember Rocky sold his share in the business and bought that big boat?'

Sky bit her lip. 'Yes, I think I remember.'

'Last year the business was sold for... I don't remember—a ton of money.'

Sky sighed. 'What's the point, Mom? What's that got to do with Rocky?'

'Oh, Sky! Rocky is here because he filed a lawsuit! He says the guy owes him and he's going to make him pay up because he cheated him when he bought his share seven years ago.'

Sky felt suddenly sick. It was like a nightmare—words, looks, thoughts, suspicions floated through her mind like pieces of a jigsaw puzzle, falling together neatly in a nightmarish picture.

'A lawsuit,' she whispered.

'Yes. Oh, Sky, I wasn't sure if I should tell you, but——'

'He's suing Chase,' she said, her voice curiously dead. And as she heard herself say the words, her life, the whole wonderful fairy-tale world she'd lived in for the past weeks came crashing down around her.

CHAPTER EIGHT

'Rocky is suing Chase,' Sky repeated, as if saying it again would make it easier to accept.

'Yes,' said her mother on the other end of the line. 'Rocky doesn't know you're working for Chase on this assignment. I haven't told him anything. I don't know...' She hesitated. 'I didn't know what there was between you and Chase...' Her voice trailed away as if she knew well enough what there was now.

Sky's knuckles were white as her hand clamped around the receiver. Oh, God, she thought, I can't bear this. Please make it not be true. Her knees shook and it was hard to breathe. 'What does Rocky say Chase did exactly?' She caught the note of hysteria in her voice and she clamped her teeth together hard.

'Sky, I...'

'Tell me, Mom! I want to know!' She hardly recognised her own voice.

'Rocky's lawyer says they're going to prove that Chase misrepresented the value of the business and its goodwill, that he swindled Rocky out of a large amount of money by taking advantage of Rocky's trust, and that he was...unscrupulous.' Her mother sounded agonised.

Sky pressed her eyes shut tight as if it could block out the words she was hearing. It couldn't be true. Something was wrong, terribly wrong. This was some horrible mistake. Why would Rocky do such a thing unless it was truly warranted? Rocky, who didn't care about money; Rocky, who was as honest as gold. It couldn't be Chase. It had to be somebody else.

'Are you sure it's Chase? Chase Montana?' she asked, her voice raw with fear.

'Yes. Chase Montana, from the Montana Group. I wanted it to be somebody else, too, Sky, but it isn't. I'm so sorry, sweetheart.'

Sky wasn't sure what she said to terminate the conversation. She sat in the chair, shaking, until suddenly tortured sobs broke loose and she collapsed in a storm of weeping.

Later that night she sat huddled on her bed, too exhausted to cry any longer. It seemed she'd shed every last tear she possessed.

It was so easy now, with the wisdom of hindsight, to see the signs, to piece it all together. She should have known something was wrong from the beginning. She *had* known something was wrong, but she'd ignored the signs because she'd fallen in love. But understanding it now didn't help; it was too late.

Years ago Chase and Rocky had been in business together somewhere in the islands. She imagined they'd met scuba-diving or sailing.

Rocky was no businessman. He loved the water and he made a somewhat haphazard living, but he was a happy man doing what he enjoyed. He'd never had much business sense and no doubt it was easy to take advantage of this. It wasn't at all difficult to imagine that Chase, with his inborn business talents, had taken advantage of her trusting brother. Business was business, after all.

She pressed her balled hands against her burning eyes. Stars exploded behind her eyelids and she released the pressure. I can't stand this, she thought desperately, hugging the pillow against her chest. I can't bear it. I have to leave. I can't stay.

The thought of staying here with Chase in the intimacy of the small cabin was intolerable. She should pack up now, get out of the house before Chase came back from entertaining the island's politicians. She did not want to face him. She did not want to see him ever again.

You can't leave, a more sober part of her said. There's a week left on your contract.

I don't care. I can't stay.

You are a professional. You have a job to do. You have a contract.

Contracts can be cancelled. It happens all the time.

You are a professional. You can't let a personal issue stand in the way of your work. Breaking a contract is not good business. It's bad for your career.

She clutched the pillow and clenched her teeth. She would face him first, then make up her mind.

It was well after ten that night when she heard the Mini Moke drive up. Moments later his footsteps moved through the living-room. Her stomach lurched, her heart contracted painfully as if some giant hand were squeezing it.

She wanted to crawl under the sheet and pretend she was sleeping, but she sat frozen on the bed, still hugging her pillow as if she could possibly derive strength from it.

Or perhaps just insulate her heart.

He came quietly into the bedroom and as he came closer to the bed he noticed her face in the light of the bedside lamp.

'Sky?' Worry coloured his voice. 'You're crying!' He was with her in a couple of giant steps, his hands coming down on her upper arms as he lowered himself on to the side of the bed. 'What's wrong?'

She froze under his touch. She wasn't sure she could talk. 'My mother called,' she said, forcing the words out with an effort. 'She told me about the lawsuit.'

He closed his eyes briefly and swore under his breath.

She shook off his hands and edged away from him. 'You deceived me!' she burst out, her voice raw with anguish. 'You deceived me from the day we met!' She was shaking and more tears ran down her face.

'No, Sky, no.'

She wiped furiously at her face with the edge of the sheet. 'Don't you dare deny it! You knew I was Rocky's sister and that's why you mistrusted me! You thought Rocky had sent me to spy on you!'

'Yes,' he said wearily. 'Of course I did.'

'You should have told me!'

He remained silent and a terrible tension filled the softly lit room.

'But you didn't tell me, did you? And I know why, Chase, I know why! You knew if you told me I'd never, *ever* have anything to do with you! And you wanted me, didn't you?' Her voice was bitter.

She wanted to hit him, hurt him, beat his chest, but she clutched the pillow to her with all her might. 'But you didn't want me for the long haul, because sooner or later I'd find out and you knew it would all be over and——'

'Sky! Stop it!' he said harshly. 'Listen to me!'

'No! Why should I listen to you now? I know why you didn't tell me! You didn't want me to know what kind of man you really are—taking advantage of people for money! Making unscrupulous business deals! Is that the way it goes when you become successful? Is it some sort of addiction? Is it never, ever enough?' She was losing control and she didn't care. All she felt was a searing pain and the words just kept on coming.

'Sky, stop it!' He was shaking her, and she burst into tears.

'I hate you!' she whispered. 'I hate what you've done to me! I hate what you've done to my brother!' She wrenched herself out of his grip. 'You're nothing but a cheap, unscrupulous swindler!'

His face grew stone-cold and his eyes froze into green ice. He stared at her for what seemed like an eternity while the silence throbbed with emotion. Then he came to his feet and strode out of the room without saying another word.

Sky's whole body was trembling and she could not get herself to calm down. All her instincts told her to get off the island as fast as possible. She should pack up her things now, drive to Port Royal, take a room at the Sugar Bay hotel and leave at the first opportunity she had in the morning.

But the professional part of her recoiled from the idea of flight. She had a contract. She had a job to do. She, Sky Malone, was not a coward.

Exhausted with emotion, she fell asleep on top of the covers, with her clothes still on, and slept straight through the night. She awoke to the jubilant chirping of birds and the smell of coffee. Her body felt as if it had been hiding in a dank cave for the major part of the century. Her limbs did not want to move and she struggled off the bed and into the shower, feeling as if she was dragging a bag of wet cement behind her.

The bathroom was full of steam and the fragrance of soap and aftershave. She slipped on the wet tiled floor and grasped the towel-rack to keep herself from falling. As she steadied herself, Chase's towel fell to the floor and she picked it up automatically. It was damp from his shower and she put it to her face on impulse. Anguish tore at her and she tossed it to the floor in furious misery. What was the matter with her?

Her throat ached and her eyes burned as she stood in the shower, willing herself not to cry, willing herself not to feel. It was the only way to survive.

Don't feel, she told herself as she dried herself off. Don't feel, don't feel, don't feel.

Mrs Drakes' 'good morning' was bright and cheerful, her face sunny and happy. Coffee and breakfast were on the terrace, she told Sky.

So was Chase, but Sky needed coffee the way a drowning man needed air, so she went to the terrace and poured herself a cup from the thermal coffee-pot, amazed at her composure, amazed at how cold she felt inside. Chase was reading the paper and was seemingly oblivious to her presence.

This was fine by her. As far as she was concerned she never wanted to see him again, nor hear his voice. Her heart was frozen. Nothing could hurt her now.

He lowered the paper as she buttered a fresh bread roll.

'You can leave as soon as you like,' he told her. 'I'll relieve you of your contractual obligations.'

She gave him a contemptuous stare. 'I came here to do a job, and I'll do it. I am a professional and I do not break my contracts.'

'Very commendable, but in the circumstances——'

'The circumstances are personal, not professional. I won't let them interfere with my work. I'll finish up the time working by myself, and then I'll go home.' She picked up the bread roll in one hand, the coffee-cup in the other, went back into the house, and into her room. She sat on the edge of the bed, drinking her coffee, wondering if she would be able to survive the next week sharing the cabin with him.

But as it happened she saw little of Chase for the following three days. They managed successfully to keep themselves occupied away from the house and away from each other. However, whenever they happened to be in the cabin at the same time, the air was arctic.

He was frigidly cold to her. She was frigidly cold to him. It was unbearable. Her nerves were strung taut and she wasn't, as it turned out, quite as frozen inside as she wanted to be.

Every time she saw him she felt as if she was dying a little more.

Paul Santelli called her the next evening while Chase was still out, and told her he was going on turtle patrol that night. There was a small nesting beach where leatherback turtles came to lay their eggs. They might just get lucky. Would she be interested in joining him tonight?

'What kind of a question is that?' she asked and he laughed.

'There are no guarantees. We may have to hang around on the beach all night for nothing, but we can try again tomorrow night as well.'

'I'll be there. Tell me where to meet you.' She wouldn't want to miss this for the world.

Paul had brought hot coffee and chocolate bars to sustain them through their nocturnal vigil. It was a lucky night. The moon was full, flooding the scene with a magic silver light. It was just before two when Sky watched in wonder as a giant leatherback turtle lumbered out of the water and began to plod through the sand towards a stand of seagrape trees.

'It's huge!' she whispered in awe. It was like something out of the dinosaur age, an ancient primitive creature labouring up the beach in the dim light of night to dig its nest. It was at least five feet long, she estimated.

'About nine hundred pounds, I'd guess,' said Paul in a low voice.

In the cover of the seagrapes, the turtle made a nest, digging in the sand with her rear flippers, sending sand flying. But once the nest was finished, she was not happy. Abandoning it, she plodded further along the stand of trees, found another spot, and started all over again.

'Why is she doing that?' Sky asked.

'We don't know,' said Paul. 'It's a mystery to science. They may make several nests before they're satisfied. When we check the nests we can't figure out why.'

The second nest proved satisfactory. The huge turtle settled into the sandy hole. Transfixed, Sky watched as a stream of shiny white, perfectly round eggs dropped into the nest. Carefully, they moved in closer.

'It's all right,' said Paul. 'Once they're laying eggs they're in some sort of trance and they don't know what goes on around them.'

In a haze of excitement, Sky took photo after photo while the turtle, as if indeed in a trance, went on depositing her eggs—more than eighty, they counted, in an hour and a half.

Sky couldn't believe her good luck. She had seen the spectacle on nature documentaries, but standing here on a tropical beach in the silver moonlight watching it happen in reality was like nothing she could have imagined. It filled her with a sense of magic and wonder.

If only Chase could have been here with me. The thought came of its own accord, unwanted. Pain stabbed at her and tears blinded her for a moment. It took all her strength to push the thought away.

Having fulfilled her maternal duties, the turtle covered up the eggs with sand and trudged back to the sea. She would never come back to the nest, according to Paul. The eggs were on their own and

would hatch in a couple of months and the tiny
baby turtles would find their way into the sea to
start the cycle of life again—at least, if someone
didn't dig up the nest and collect the eggs for food.
Finding a turtle nest was dead easy. All you had to
do was come in the morning and find the turtle
tracks the mother had left in the sand. So Sky and
Paul obliterated the tracks and tried to obscure the
nest as much as possible. Then, tired and elated,
they wished each other good morning and went
their separate ways.

Exhilarated and hyped up on coffee and chocolate bars, Sky drove back to the cabin, the balmy,
fragrant night air blowing in her face, the dark
world around her full of secrets and mysteries.

She'd slipped out of the house at twelve mid-
night after Chase had gone to bed. Arriving back,
she parked the car a short distance from the cabin
and walked the rest of the way. She'd intended to
slip in as quietly as possible and not awaken Chase,
but as she rounded the bend and the cottage came
into view her heart lurched and she knew that her
efforts had been wasted.

The light was on in the main room and as she
quietly moved across the terrace she saw Chase
sitting on the sofa, the coffee-table strewn with
papers, a coffee-cup and a half-empty glass at his
elbow. He looked tired and his hair hung over his
forehead.

'Where the hell have you been all night?' he demanded, his voice harsh and furious. He rose to
his feet, towering over her. His face seemed carved
out of stone and his cold green eyes raked over her
from head to toe.

All the joy and elation of the night evaporated in the heat of his rage. Sky felt herself begin to tremble, felt her own anger take over. Who was he to ask her what she did at night?

She glared up at him. 'With Paul,' she said coldly, knowing full well what he would think, and not caring, wanting to hurt him.

His jaw clenched hard. His eyes took in her sandy feet and legs, her damp and rumpled shorts and shirt. 'Frolicking on the beach?' he said with icy contempt. 'Or did you find some interesting variety of nocturnal lizard to study?'

'It's none of your business what I do with my nights.' Her voice shook, but she forced herself to look straight into his face. She would not allow him to intimidate her. He had no right to question her.

He grimaced with distaste. 'I thought you had more class,' he said with chilling disdain. 'Is this some perverted sort of revenge?'

'Revenge?' She laughed coldly. 'Oh, please, don't be so melodramatic.' She pushed her hair off her forehead and took a step forward. 'Now, if you'll excuse me, I'd like to go inside and have a shower.'

He did not move to let her pass. Instead he took her upper arms in an iron grip.

'Why?' he ground out. 'Why in God's name do you waste yourself on some itinerant lizard freak?' His face worked and the searing anguish in his eyes shook her to the core. It made everything else fade into the background—the whole sorry affair—all the hurt and anger. All she could see was the raw pain in his eyes; all she could hear was the torment in his voice.

Her throat felt gritty and she swallowed hard. 'I don't sleep around,' she said huskily. 'I was at the beach with Paul taking pictures of a leatherback turtle laying her eggs. I was working.' She shook herself free, and without looking at him she marched into her room and threw herself on the bed, sand and all. She pressed her face into the pillow and willed herself not to cry.

Just when she thought the situation could not get worse, it did. Arriving home a little after five the next afternoon, Sky found two visitors sitting on the terrace. One was a dark-haired woman she didn't know. The other was a blond man she knew very well: her brother Rocky, complete with lurid flowered shirt and wicked grin.

'Hey! Blue Sky!' She was lifted off her feet and wrapped in a bear hug that squeezed the air out of her lungs. Emotion washed over her—joy at seeing Rocky, panic at seeing Rocky.

'Rocky!' she cried after she'd caught her breath. 'What are you doing here?'

He set her back on her feet and grinned down at her with laughing blue eyes. 'I came to see you! What else? Did you think I was going back to the other end of the world without seeing my little sister?' He gave her a wounded look. 'Besides, I wanted you to meet Tiffany.'

The woman came to her feet and smiled. She was of medium height, with short curly brown hair and warm brown eyes. She wore white shorts and a turquoise shirt and had a healthy, athletic look.

'Meet Tiffany,' he said. 'Tiff, my sister Sky.'

They shook hands, smiling curiously at each other. 'Sit down,' said Sky. 'Can I get you another drink?' The glasses on the table indicated that Mrs Drakes had seen to them once already.

'Yes, please,' they said. Moments later they were drinking tangy, sour sop juice and talking. Sky prayed silently that Chase wouldn't come back until she'd found a way to get rid of the pair.

This was a nightmare. How was she going to deal with this?

'How did you get here?' she asked, and Rocky told her they'd borrowed her father's old pick-up truck, driven to Miami, parked it in a friend's driveway, taken a flight to St John's, borrowed a cabin cruiser from another friend and here they were. The taxi driver had known just where to find her; no problem at all.

'So tell me about this guy you're working for,' said Rocky, leaning back in his chair, sipping his drink with lazy contentment.

Her body tensed. 'You don't need me to tell you about him. You know who he is,' she said tightly. 'Surely Mom told you?'

His face darkened. 'Yes.'

'This is very awkward, your being here,' she said. 'You understand that, don't you?'

He nodded. 'But we wanted to see you.' He glanced around. 'Interesting place, but not what I had expected,' he commented.

She gulped her drink nervously. 'What had you expected?'

'A luxurious villa—swimming-pool, tennis courts, Roman statues in the garden, the works.'

Well, she couldn't blame him. That was what she had expected as well.

'I want to know about the lawsuit,' she said, meeting his eyes. 'And about that business you had with him years ago.'

He put his glass down. 'It was a great business. We did very well.' He sighed. 'Just think of it; if I'd stayed in the game I could have been rich now too.'

'You don't want to be rich,' stated Tiffany promptly.

He grinned at her. 'Ah, you know me so well.' He grimaced. 'Just think of all the bookkeeping, the bank statements, the investments! The decisions! What a nightmare!'

'That's what I thought you'd say,' Tiffany said drily.

'I'm glad you're so understanding. It's nice to know you're not marrying me for my money.'

Sky gaped. 'You're getting married?' She could not believe what she was hearing. Rocky was not the marrying type, or so he had said for many years.

Rocky nodded, his blue eyes sparking with humour. 'It's a miracle, Sky. I didn't think there was a woman on this earth who would want to put up with my vagabond ways.' He reached out and took Tiffany's hand in his big brown one. He grinned triumphantly. 'Guess what? I found another vagabond.'

Tiffany just smiled. As Sky remembered her mother mentioning, Tiffany was not one for many words, which was just as well. Rocky could talk enough for two.

Sky swallowed. 'Well, my congratulations.'

'Thank you.'

Sky looked again at Tiffany. 'We'll be sisters-in-law.' It was an odd feeling, somehow, but then she'd had no time to get used to the idea. And she didn't even know this woman.

Tiffany smiled. 'I'm looking forward to it.' She glanced around as she took another drink of her juice. 'I like this place. Fits in nicely with the surroundings, as if it's meant to be here.'

'Yes,' said Sky, feeling a painful lump form in her throat. 'It was designed that way.' She looked back at Rocky and steeled herself. 'I want to know how Chase cheated you.'

Tiffany studied her drink. Rocky looked pained. 'Not now,' he said. 'It's a nasty business and I'm enjoying being here.' He scrutinised her. 'Are you nervous about something?'

'Of course I'm nervous! What if Chase sees you here? He'll be home soon.'

He waved his hand as if to dismiss her fears. 'I'll handle it, Sky. Don't worry about it.'

His casual attitude irritated her. 'He doesn't like you and he's bigger than you are.'

His blond brows shot up. 'What does that mean?'

'Oh, for heaven's sake, Rocky, use your imagination!'

And then she heard the Mini Moke bump up the unpaved track. She froze in her chair as she watched Chase leap out of the little car. He wore a lightweight suit, a shirt and tie. He strode up to the terrace, and as his eyes caught sight of Rocky Sky saw his features turn to stone. His eyes narrowed dangerously as he took the last few steps to reach the terrace.

Rocky came to his feet. For an interminable moment the two men faced each other in silence. Then Rocky extended his hand.

'Hello, Chase,' he said.

CHAPTER NINE

SKY'S heart thundered in her chest as she watched the two men. Chase's face was glacial as he looked at Rocky. Demonstratively, he pushed his jacket aside and slipped his hands in his trouser pockets.

'You've got a lot of gall coming here,' he said in a low, controlled voice that sent a shiver down her back.

Rocky crossed his arms in front of his chest. 'I thought maybe we could handle our differences personally and settle out of court,' he said calmly.

Chase gave him a look of icy contempt. 'You've got to be deranged. Now get the hell out of my house.' He strode into the cottage without another word.

Trembling all over, Sky expelled a long breath and looked at Rocky and Tiffany. Rocky made a rueful grimace.

'The emperor is displeased. I suppose we'd better leave.'

'Is your cruiser in the marina at Port Royal?' Sky asked, her voice unsteady.

He nodded and reached out his hand to help Tiffany out of her chair. 'Yes. The taxi is waiting for us down the hill, at that food stall.' He grinned his boyish grin. 'I had no illusions about being invited to partake in a celebratory dinner here tonight, Sky.' He gave her a hug. 'Don't look so stricken. Relax. Can you come sailing with us tomorrow?'

The temptation was great, but she shook her head. 'I have work to do.'

'Come afterward, for drinks and dinner,' invited Tiffany.

'I'd love to,' said Sky.

They said goodbye and Sky watched the two as they walked down the track and disappeared around the bend. Then she went inside, her heart in her throat, her nerves jangling. Moments later Chase came out of his room, having changed into khaki shorts and a black T-shirt. His eyes were a cold, hard green.

'Did you invite them here?' he demanded.

'No, I did not! Why would I do that?'

He shrugged. 'God knows.'

She was shaking with anger. 'He wants to settle your differences and you call him deranged! What is the matter with you?'

'Maybe you should ask what's the matter with him,' he said with cold disdain. 'Maybe you should ask yourself why he's suddenly so eager to get this suit out of the way.'

She put her hands on her hips. 'Why don't you tell me?'

His laugh was short and humourless. 'You wouldn't like what I had to say. Just let me assure you that he'll come out a loser in this deal, no matter what he tries.' A muscle jerked in his face. 'And in case it matters to you, that will make three of us.' He strode back into his bedroom and slammed the door shut. A baby lizard fell out of the thatch and scuttled away behind the bookcase in terror.

The next day passed in a blur and keeping her mind on her work was a struggle. She found herself sitting aimlessly under a tree or on a rock, staring blindly into nothing, her camera forgotten in her lap.

'So, what's going on, Sky?' Rocky asked when she arrived at the cruiser. It was a big, luxurious yacht and Sky couldn't help but smile in amazement. He'd borrowed this boat as easily as if it were a hammer or a drill. Rocky had friends the world over, friends who respected his skills and knew their luxury toys were in good hands with him, friends who owed him a favour or two, no doubt, because Rocky spent half his life doing favours for people or helping them out in some fashion or other.

Rocky pushed her down in a chair and a minute later Tiffany handed her a rum punch.

'Thanks.' She took a sip of the drink.

'You didn't answer my question,' said Rocky. 'What's going on with you?'

'Nothing.' She shrugged lightly and glanced out over the tiny marina. 'Nothing is going on. I'm on a job. I'll be done next week and then I'll go home.'

'What about Chase?'

'What about him?'

His blue eyes met hers. 'You love him,' he said quietly.

She grimaced at him. 'Please don't give me the warning speech. I know all about what he is, so don't worry about me. I'll get over it.' She tried to sound convincing, but she wasn't sure if she'd pulled it off. She took another drink.

Rocky frowned. 'I don't like seeing you get over things.'

'I'm a big girl now, Rocky.' She gave him a half-smile. 'No death-defying adventures necessary.'

Tiffany came out of the galley with a tray of food, which she placed on a small table. Dinner was delicious, and the conversation remained mercifully light.

It was a nice evening and Sky felt her spirits lift as she listened to Rocky's scintillating accounts of his travels. He had a talent for drama and could make even the most mundane of occurrences sound like an exhilarating adventure. It felt good to laugh again and feel light-hearted, even if for a few hours.

'I need to talk to Chase,' said Rocky as she got ready to leave. 'I'm not crazy about this lawsuit business. It's taking forever, and I have no desire to hang around Virginia for months on end. I've got things to do.' He stirred sugar into his coffee. 'I'll drop by again tomorrow night and see if he's in a more amiable mood.'

Sky gave a short laugh. 'You've got to be kidding, Rocky.'

'No, I'm not,' he said evenly.

Tiffany had said nothing, but it was obvious that she'd been taking in every word. It was also obvious that she was annoyed at Rocky. Sky wondered why.

The next evening Rocky arrived at the cabin as he had said he would. Sky and Chase had just finished a silent dinner when Sky noticed Rocky stride up on the terrace.

'I need to talk to you,' he said to Chase.

'Talk to my lawyer,' said Chase, tossing his napkin on the table and rising to his feet.

'I'm sick of lawyers,' said Rocky with disgust, 'and that includes my own. I'd like to invite you and my sister to dinner at the Sugar Bay hotel in town tomorrow night.'

Chase gave a scornful little laugh. 'You're joking.'

Rocky crossed his arms in front of his chest. 'No, I'm not joking.'

Chase put his hands on his hips and surveyed Rocky as if he were some unwelcome rodent. 'Running scared, perhaps?'

Rocky gave an amused little smile. 'No, I am not running scared, Chase.'

Sky sat motionless in her chair. There was a silence, broken only by the pounding of her heart. She looked at Chase. He was studying Rocky with narrowed eyes, a look of calculation on his face.

'This ought to be good,' he said in a low voice. 'Dinner, the four of us. I assume your lady friend will be along?'

'Yes.'

Chase turned to Sky, one eyebrow cocked. 'And what do you think of this cosy arrangement?'

Her hands clenched into fists. 'If my brother has something to say to you, you ought to give him the courtesy of listening.'

He gave her a mocking look. 'The same courtesy you failed to extend me when I wanted you to listen to me?'

Heat flushed her face. 'You deceived me! What were you going to tell me? That it wasn't true——?'

'Excuse me,' said Rocky politely, interrupting her. 'I'll be at the hotel restaurant at seven tomorrow night.' He looked Chase straight in the face. 'I'd appreciate it if you would come.'

Chase's mouth curled. 'I can't wait,' he said.

The next day, after coming home from roaming the island on her own, Sky stayed in her room until it was time to go. Dressed in a short summer dress, she emerged, car keys in hand, to find Chase sitting on the terrace, reading a newspaper. Her body tense, she moved past him and he put the paper down.

'We'll go together,' he said, rising to his feet.

Her stomach churned. It made no sense to take two cars, of course, but sitting next to him for even the short drive would do her nervous system no good.

They drove in a nerve-racking silence through the darkened landscape. She stared out over the sea, seeing the glitter of some far-off lights from a cruiser.

Rocky and Tiffany were already at the table. Tiffany looked nice in a simple dress, her hair shiny, her face made up only lightly. A calm serenity emanated from her. As if she'd figured out the world and how to live in it. Sky envied her her composure and wished she could feel calm herself. She felt like a wreck. Her stomach was tied into knots and she wasn't sure she'd be able to eat.

'Good evening,' said Chase politely—too politely. He held out a chair for Sky and she sat down.

He settled himself on a chair as well.

'How about a drink?' offered Rocky.

Drinks were ordered.

'I like this place,' Rocky remarked casually, glancing around. 'It has atmosphere, ambience.'

It was an old hotel dating from colonial times and the furnishings looked as if they'd been there forever. The upholstery was threadbare, as was the faded red carpeting. Old-fashioned paintings depicting pastoral scenes adorned the walls. The dining-room was full of faded glory, but the table-cloths were pristine white and the view of the harbour was wonderful. A waning moon illuminated the water and lights glimmered from a few small boats.

'It has real character,' said Tiffany. 'Not the sort of fake tourist stuff you see everywhere these days.'

Chase sat drinking his drink, saying nothing. He was studying Tiffany, his look calculating, as if he wondered what she was doing there.

Sky gulped her wine. She was going too fast. She made herself sip it.

Rocky picked up his menu. 'So, let's see what the scoop is on food here.'

They discussed food. It was all very civilised. Chase was silent, his eyes dark and unreadable.

'How's the flying fish in this place?' asked Rocky, looking at Chase.

'I'm sure it's excellent,' he said coldly.

They ordered food and a bottle of wine.

'What I'd like to do,' said Rocky, looking at Chase, 'is retrace our relationship and recap the main points of what led to this—er—conflict. Let's see, it was eight years ago that you and I met on St John's.'

Chase stared at him stonily and said nothing.

'You'd just finished Harvard, and you were looking for some good fun.'

Again, Chase said nothing. He leaned back in his chair, sipping his drink, apparently content to let Rocky do the talking.

Rocky examined his drink, frowning as if concentrating. 'We sailed, we fished, we dived. I had a sailing boat, and we started giving lessons, taking out tourists. You bought a boat for yourself. Pretty soon we were doing well. We ploughed in a little more money.' He gave Chase a narrow-eyed look. 'Stop me any time you feel like it, partner.'

Chase's mouth twisted sardonically. 'You are doing just fine, so far.'

'Good. A year later we had a real business. Small, but respectable. Would you agree?'

Chase gave a slight nod. A waiter appeared at their table, his presence defusing the tension slightly as he handed them their food and asked if anything else was needed.

Valium, said Sky silently. She stared at her plate and forced herself to take a bite from the poached parrot fish.

'May I have the salt, please?' asked Tiffany, and she smiled at Sky. There was something in her eyes, some message that Sky wasn't sure she understood. Some sort of reassurance. She handed Tiffany the salt.

'This is excellent,' said Rocky pleasantly. Sky wanted to kick him under the table. She felt murderously angry. What game was he playing at here?

Why couldn't he just come out and propose whatever deal he wanted to make?

'Well,' Rocky went on amiably, 'as I said, we were doing very well. We were having fun. A lot of fun. But fun was not enough for you—you wanted to make more money and develop the place into some super nature resort and play the big game. Of course, having an MBA from Harvard, you would look at things that way. I respect that.'

Sky cast a furious look at him. He grinned back at her. There was a gleam in his eyes that promised nothing good. She recognised it from their childhood days.

Chase went on eating.

Rocky took a drink from his wine. 'Needless to say, I had no such aspirations. I didn't want to be tied down and get so involved in running a business I'd forget to enjoy the small pleasures of life. I wanted to be able to pack up on short notice and find greener pastures, or, rather, bluer waters. I had dreams of going to the Fiji islands.' He took another drink. 'How am I doing?' he asked again.

'Oh, please continue. It's riveting,' said Chase with biting sarcasm.

'Good. I wouldn't want you to be bored. And it gets better yet.'

Sky noticed that Tiffany kicked Rocky under the table. She pretended to be occupied with her food, but she was annoyed.

'All right. So, we decided that perhaps we ought to make a deal and you would buy me out. This would leave me free to go where I wanted to go, and it would leave you free to build up the business as you saw fit. A perfect solution.' He smiled affably. 'So, you bought me out. I had money, got myself a new boat and sailed to Fiji.'

And this, of course, should have been the end of the story, but it hadn't been. Sky swallowed another bite, not tasting it. The tension made her feel brittle.

'Last year you sold the business,' Rocky continued. 'It's quite a place now, very big. I read about it in a magazine. I talked with friends about my having been involved in the start-up. Needless to say they were quite impressed. We were having a few drinks and discussed the situation. Somebody expressed the opinion that I'd made a mistake selling out. We drank some more. The idea of me being rich seemed suddenly very appealing to us. We talked some more. The consensus was that I had not received enough money for my share of the business. I decided to look into it and one of my friends was willing to help me figure this out.'

'It's amazing what a bunch of drunk friends won't do for you,' said Chase caustically.

'Right,' said Rocky, unperturbed. 'Soon we had a lawyer involved and things got rather exciting.'

Chase's face was livid, but he said nothing.

'Somebody did a little research into your company and things got a little more exciting.'

Sky sat motionless, unable to eat another bite. She had the horrible vision of Chase getting up from the table and socking Rocky in the mouth right there in the middle of the restaurant.

'In fact,' said Rocky slowly, 'things were getting so exciting, and so many people were getting involved, that I was beginning to lose track of what was going on.' He smiled suddenly and glanced over at Tiffany. 'Tiffany, however, has a very cool head on her shoulders and was not impressed by the party atmosphere of the situation. She decided to take matters in hand.'

'Skip it, sailor,' said Tiffany. 'Get to the point.'

'I'm not going to skip it.' He speared a piece of breadfruit fritter and ate it. 'She looked over all the original paperwork, as well as all the rest of the paperwork. Did I tell you she runs her own business? Anyway, her findings were rather interesting.'

'I haven't heard anything interesting yet,' said Chase contemptuously. 'How about you cut the dramatics here?' He pushed his empty plate aside. 'You have five more minutes. If you have anything worthwhile to say, I suggest you do it now.'

Rocky nodded. 'Right.'

For the first time that evening, Sky noticed a certain hesitation in him. Her heart was throbbing wildly. He'd indicated that he wanted to resolve the conflict, but she had no idea how. 'He'll come out a loser in this deal, no matter what he tries. And in case it matters to you, that will make three of us.' Chase's words of the other day rang in her head.

Rocky wiped his mouth with a napkin. 'As you said, it is amazing what a bunch of drunk friends won't do for you. And it's amazing what an idiot a normally sane person can make of himself.' Rocky looked straight at Chase. 'There was no cause for me to think you cheated me out of money by giving me a bad deal. You didn't.'

CHAPTER TEN

THE silence at the table was electric. Sky sat frozen as she took in the scene, not sure she was conscious, not sure this was not some weird, mixed-up dream. Chase looked back at Rocky and said nothing. His face was expressionless, his body still.

Rocky played with his fork. 'I made a bad mistake and I apologise. I will make a public statement to that effect.' He glanced at Sky, a plea in his eyes. 'I'm sorry,' he said.

Sky felt dizzy with a sudden frightening rage and a force outside herself took over. She came shakily to her feet and glared at Rocky.

'You bastard!' she whispered fiercely. 'I *believed* you! I *trusted* you!'

She didn't know how she managed to make her legs move, but the next thing she knew she was in the old-fashioned ladies' cloakroom, curled up in a red upholstered chair, shaking so badly that her teeth were chattering.

The door opened and Tiffany came in, her face worried. 'Are you all right?' she asked softly.

'No, I'm not all right!' Her voice shook.

'I'm sorry, Sky.'

'It's not your fault.'

'This whole sorry affair messed things up between you and Chase, didn't it?' Tiffany asked.

'Yes.' Sky's eyes flooded with tears and she drew in a shuddering breath.

'Maybe you can talk about it with him. He's waiting to take you home.'

Chase, waiting for her.

'I can't face him, Tiffany, I can't!' She began to cry and she couldn't stop herself. The anguish was too much to contain.

'Why not?'

'I mistrusted him! I told him he was a crook and took advantage of my wonderful, trusting brother. My *brother*!' She broke into more sobs. 'I *love* Rocky. I'd go through *fire* for him! I trusted and believed him! How could he *do* this to me?'

Tiffany slowly shook her head. 'He didn't do it to you, Sky. He didn't even know you were involved with Chase until your mother told him. He was mortified.'

'Good! He should have been! How could he have ever done such a stupid thing? He doesn't even care about money!'

Tiffany handed her some tissues. 'It wasn't the money, Sky. It was his pride. He didn't like to think he'd been made a fool of by some Harvard guy. He listened to the wrong people and he used bad judgement. We all do at times.'

Sky grimaced. She could say amen to that. She herself had won the grand prize for the season. She wiped at her eyes and blew her nose, but the tears just kept coming. 'What I did to Chase was unforgivable,' she sobbed. 'I *love* him, Tiffany. And then I turned on him. I *mistrusted* him. What kind of love is that?'

'Imperfect,' said Tiffany. A smile warmed her eyes. 'Oh, Sky, not even love is perfect. We learn as we go along. We have to forgive ourselves and each other and go on.'

Sky gazed at Tiffany's face and for a moment she was distracted. 'Where ever did Rocky find you?' she asked and Tiffany gave a low laugh.

'On a sailing boat, where else?'

'And you love him?'

'Yes, I love him. For all his childish love of drama, for all his faults, he is the most honest, loving and loyal man I know. What he did to Chase was really stupid.' She shrugged. 'I've done a couple of really stupid things myself.'

It was hard to believe. Tiffany seemed so down-to-earth, so calm.

'And when Rocky realised he was wrong,' Tiffany went on, 'he owned up to it and took responsibility. I can't say I was thrilled with the way he did it. He has to make a show out of everything, but then, that's the way he is.'

Sky could only admire her. At this very moment she could not imagine any woman wanting to put up with Rocky and his theatrics.

'He's lucky to have you,' Sky said, and meant it.

'I'm lucky to have him.' Tiffany got up. 'Come on; splash some water on your face.'

Not that it would do much good. Her face was red and puffy. Sky groaned as she looked at herself in the mirror and fresh tears blurred her eyes. This was no way to face Chase. She needed time to think.

'I can't go home with Chase now,' she said thickly. I can't face him.'

'If he loves you, he'll understand.'

It sounded very noble, but all Sky could see was Chase's frigid face in her mind's eye. She wasn't so sure he would understand, or forgive. A shudder went through her. 'I need time to think.'

'Do you want to stay on the boat with us?'

Sky shook her head. 'I don't want to see Rocky, either. I might punch his lights out.' It was an expression she'd picked up from her mother's preschoolers.

Tiffany gave a half-smile. 'I'll do it for you. Where are you going to stay tonight?'

'I don't know. Here, I guess. I don't care. Please, just tell Chase I'm not coming back with him. Make something up.'

The little second-storey room had a bare wooden floor, faded flowered curtains and a thin, fraying bedspread. The mattress was too soft and the iron bedstead creaked as she lay down. It didn't matter; all she cared about was being alone.

And she was alone now in this spartan little room. A breeze from the sea gently stirred the curtains. The laughter of a woman floated up from the street. Trying to clear her mind, Sky focused on an old-fashioned picture on the wall depicting a barefoot, smiling slave girl with a bucket of water on her head. The picture must have hung there for a hundred and fifty years or so. It was probably worth a small fortune and nobody even knew it.

She fell asleep, waking restlessly several times during the night, haunted by visions of Chase's cold, contemptuous eyes. She felt miserable and small and unworthy. She loved him and she had failed him. She had even refused to listen to him.

The next morning she had a shower and dressed in the clothes she'd put on clean the night before to go out to dinner, and decided they'd have to last her for the day. When she'd signed in last night, the girl behind the desk had found her a toothbrush and toothpaste; she'd manage to do without the rest of her things.

After breakfast she roamed the small town, wishing she could just get on a plane and leave. She had money and a credit card, but her passport, her clothes, her cameras and other photographic equipment were all at the cabin.

Maybe she should go back to the cottage in the hope that he wouldn't be there, pack her things and depart on the next puddle-jumper out.

But she couldn't leave just like that. She'd made a mistake and she should own up to it. As Rocky did, came the unbidden thought, and a wave of anger washed over her thinking about her brother.

She went to the open-air market, but she was too absorbed to find pleasure in the cheerful festival of colour and sound and smell. She wandered around in a daze, not really seeing, or hearing, as if her senses were drugged. All she could see was Chase's face. All she could think of was how much she loved him, how terribly wrong she had been not to trust him. How could she have shown so little trust, so little loyalty to the man she loved?

She owed him an apology. Oh, God. Her stomach twisted itself into knots just thinking about it. 'I hate you!' she'd said. 'You're nothing but a cheap, unscrupulous swindler!' How did anyone apologise for words like that? How could she apologise for such an overwhelming lack of trust?

She forgot to eat lunch and when hunger finally caught up with her she snacked on roasted plantain from a roadside stall.

She spent an hour sitting on a small terrace sipping a sorrel soda and finally made her way back to the Sugar Bay hotel where she sat in the small bar and had a rum punch to fortify her for the evening ahead. She tried to think of what to say to Chase, but all she could come up with was, I'm sorry. It didn't seem nearly adequate.

Finally, she slipped off the stool and went into the small lobby to see if someone could tell her how to find Mum's taxi, but when she arrived at the desk the front door opened and Chase entered.

Her heart slammed against her ribs and the breath stuck in her throat. The girl behind the desk gave her a worried look as she handed Sky a folded piece of paper. 'A message for you,' she said.

Chase was beside her in a few long strides. 'I thought you might want to come back,' he said without inflexion.

She swallowed. 'I was just looking for the taxi.' She stared at his chin, feeling as if at any moment now she would shatter into a thousand pieces. Why had he come to find her? The paper crumpled in her tightening fingers.

'I've got the car here.'

She followed him without speaking, slid into the passenger seat and stared blindly ahead.

'Read your note,' he said.

She turned to face him. 'Is it from you?'

'No.' He put the key in the ignition but didn't turn it.

She smoothed the wadded-up paper on her knee, turning it to catch the light from the hotel's front door. 'I never meant to hurt you. Please forgive me. Rocky.'

It was amazingly succinct for Rocky. She would have understood a page or two; instead there were only two lines. Words had even failed him.

'It's from Rocky,' she said dully. 'He wants me to forgive him.'

'Are you going to?'

No, she wanted to say. Not in a hundred years. She bit her lip and her throat ached with the effort not to cry. 'He's my brother,' she said thickly. 'I love my brother.'

Chase started the engine and they moved into the busy street. People were walking everywhere, talking, laughing. Reggae music spilled out of a rum bar. The spicy scent of food cooking floated in the air. There was joy and happiness all around and inside all she felt was despair.

They drove down the coastal road in silence, and the pain inside her only grew worse. Tears were silently running down her cheeks and she kept her face averted. The wind blew around her hair and face, chilling her wet cheeks.

When she couldn't stand it any longer she turned to look at him. It was hard to distinguish his features in the darkness.

'I'm sorry,' she said, her voice thick with tears. 'I don't know what else to say but that I'm sorry.'

'I'm sorry too,' he returned. His voice was calm and even. He turned off the road and parked the car in a small clearing which overlooked a cove below. The white crescent of sand glistened in the moonlight and the placid sea shimmered darkly.

'I apologise for my brother and the problems he caused you,' she said.

'You have no reason to apologise for your brother. He did so quite adequately himself.'

'This affair must have cost your company all kinds of time and money,' she said.

He shrugged. 'We have our own legal department and it's all part of doing business. It was a ridiculous case and had it ever come to court it would have been over very quickly. I wasn't ever worried about that after I figured out what was going on.' He paused and met her eyes. 'I wasn't worried about losing money, Sky, or about anything to do with the case itself. I was worried about losing you.'

'Losing me?' she whispered.

'Yes. All I wanted was to get out of this mess with you still loving me.'

She felt fresh tears come to her eyes. 'But why didn't you tell me? Why didn't you tell me how it was?'

His mouth twisted bitterly. 'The only way to do that was to put your brother in a bad light. I couldn't do that. You love him. You're such a loyal sister, Sky, it's touching. I couldn't destroy that. I was hoping we could settle this affair without you knowing about it, which only proves how crazy I was in my thinking. I was desperate.'

'Desperate?'

He gave a crooked smile. 'You bowled me over the night of the party. From the moment I saw you in that parrot dress. There was something wonderfully fresh and real about you and I had never experienced such instant attraction in my life.' He paused, then, 'It frightened the hell out of me,' he added on a low note. 'It was irrational and crazy and uncontrollable. I fought it with all that I was worth, but it was hopeless.' He stroked her hair. 'I wanted you, Sky. I wanted you more than I'd wanted anything in my life, only...' He sighed.

'Only what?'

'Only there was Rocky, your beloved brother, suing me for unscrupulous business dealings. I wanted time. The more time I had, the more opportunity I had to show you who I was, for you to get to know me. Without that I never had a chance.'

Tears ran hot down her cheeks. 'I said such horrible things to you,' she whispered. 'I feel so awful.'

'I felt pretty awful myself,' he said wryly.

'I failed you.' She pressed her hands against her eyes, trying to stem the flow of tears. It felt as if she'd cried for days, as if there would never be an end to her tears.

He went on stroking her hair. 'You stood by your brother. I admire that kind of loyalty and love; it's a beautiful thing and it's part of you, of your nature.'

'I didn't show you any loyalty!'

He gave a rueful smile. 'Why should you? I'm a recovered juvenile disaster. I made my parents miserable. I broke the law. I'm a suspicious bastard. Why should you believe me over your own flesh and blood, over a brother you've known all your life, who helped you build your house, who took care of you in a time of crisis?'

'Because I love you! I should have trusted you!' she sobbed. New tears ran down her face. 'I don't understand myself any more. I should have listened to you.' She wiped furiously at her wet face. 'There has to be trust. You can't have a good relationship without trust!'

'Trust doesn't just happen, Sky. Trust has to be earned. It takes time. I hadn't yet earned your trust and that was something I had to come to terms with. My pride took a beating, but I'll live.'

'I should at least have listened to you!'

'In times of stress, reason sometimes fails us. You've known Rocky a whole lot longer than me.'

'How can you be so understanding?' she wailed. 'Why aren't you angry with me?'

He took her hand and smiled. 'Oh, I was; believe me, I was. But I had time to think. After my fury had calmed and I could think straight again, I came to see things a little differently. You'd had a number of reasons not to trust men, and deep down you were still very much afraid that things would go wrong once more, and when this happened you subconsciously decided, Here we go again. Your reaction wasn't so strange. In fact, it made perfect sense.'

'You were so angry,' she whispered.

'Of course I was. I am a proud man. Your accusations offended me deeply, especially coming from the woman I love. But I'll get over it, you know.'

'You talk as if you still love me,' she said dully.

'I do, Sky.' He gave a low laugh and drew her into his arms. 'I can't help it,' he said softly, kissing her eyes, her cheeks, her mouth. 'Even while I was furious with you I still loved you. It's my destiny. You might as well accept it because there's nothing you can do to change it.'

She felt the warmth of his body against her, the familiar scent of him, and love and relief and gratitude overwhelmed her. Tears flooded her eyes and he kissed them away.

'I want to spend the rest of my life with you,' he went on. 'You're alive and warm and loving and you care about things that matter. You're the only woman in the world I want to dream with, to plan my future with.'

'I don't understand it,' she said shakily.

'You don't have to. Just accept it. It's love; it's magic.'

She smiled against the warmth of his neck.

'Do you love me?' he asked.

She lifted her face to his. 'Yes, oh, yes! Forever and ever.'

He smiled. 'Will you please marry me?'

Joy threatened to make her cry again. 'Yes,' she whispered, feeling giddy with elation.

He kissed her and it was the most beautiful, loving kiss that said more than a thousand words could ever do. He released her mouth and took her hand in his and then with breathless surprise she felt him slide a ring on to her finger. She stared at it, dumbstruck. Even in the sparse light the diamond sparkled and glittered.

'Oh, Chase,' she whispered. 'It's beautiful!' She glanced up at his shadowed face. 'When did you get that?'

'Last week in Barbados, the day your mother called.'

Her heart contracted. 'Oh, no,' she whispered, mortified. 'Oh, Chase, I——'

He touched her lips with his finger. 'Shh...it doesn't matter any more. It's over now.'

She bit her lip and looked down at the sparkling jewel on her finger. 'It's beautiful,' she said again, and it was. Beautiful and big and gorgeous and utterly impractical and much too elegant a thing for her and it made her smile with delight. It wasn't the sort of thing to have on your finger when you were crawling through the mud or climbing rocks.

'And I bought you this, too.' He pressed a little velvet box in her hands. She opened it, feeling laughter bubble up in her throat. It was another ring—a plain gold band, solid and shiny.

'More your style, isn't it?' he asked.

She laughed. 'Yes.'

'This one is for crawling through swamps and climbing trees and hanging around on beaches at night taking pictures of prehistoric creatures laying their eggs.'

Her heart cramped. 'Did you really think I was spending the night sleeping with another man?' she asked huskily.

'Not in my rational mind. But I wasn't rational. I was insane. It was the worst night of my life.'

'You looked awful.'

He smiled ruefully. 'So awful, you told me the truth. That was when I knew not everything was lost. If you hadn't had any feelings left for me, you would have let me think the unthinkable.'

'I still loved you too,' she said softly.

'I guess it's just hopeless, then,' he said with a grin. 'We'll just have to keep on doing it forever and ever, because nothing can make us stop.'

She nodded, swallowing at the contraction in her throat.

He took her hand and grinned down at the diamond. 'As long as you wear the gold band, I don't care if you never wear this ring. It's quite an ostentatious thing, but I couldn't resist. I wanted you to have a diamond. I wanted to *give* you a diamond, for all the usual standard, sentimental reasons, I suppose.'

'You're a romantic,' she whispered, smiling.

'Yes.' He kissed her. 'And will you come home now and come to bed with me so we can make passionate love and dream up beautiful plans for the future?'

She nodded yes, but her throat was closed and tears welled up again. He kissed her and wiped her tears from her face.

'There's a condition, though. You've got to stop crying. I can't make love to a crying woman.'

'I'm just happy.'

'I know. So am I.' He kissed her quickly and then he started the engine and drove home to the cabin.

They made passionate love and dreamed wonderful dreams all through the night.

THREE LOVE STORIES..

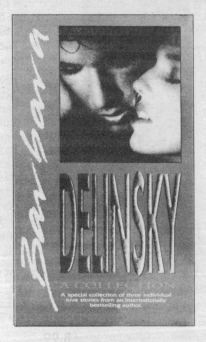

A beautiful collection of three individual love stories from *New York Times* bestselling author Barbara Delinsky – each featuring the charming and irrepressible matchmaker, Victoria Lesser.

A very collectable volume, offering new fans the chance to sample some of Delinsky's earlier work and for long-time fans collect an edition to treasure.

WORLDWIDE

AVAILABLE FROM SEPTEMBER   **PRICED £4.99**

Available from WH Smith, John Menzies, Volume One, Forbuoys, Martins, Woolworths, Tesco, Asda, Safeway and other paperback stockists.

Cruel Legacy

One man's untimely death deprives a wife of her husband, robs a man of his job and offers someone else the chance of a lifetime...

Suicide — the only way out for Andrew Ryecart, facing crippling debt. An end to his troubles, but for those he leaves behind the problems are just beginning, as the repercussions of this most desperate of acts reach out and touch the lives of six different people — changing them forever.

Special large-format paperback edition

OCTOBER
£8.99

WORLDWIDE

Next Month's Romances

Each month you can choose from a wide variety of romance with Mills & Boon. Below are the new titles to look out for next month, why not ask either Mills & Boon Reader Service or your Newsagent to reserve you a copy of the titles you want to buy — just tick the titles you would like and either post to Reader Service or take it to any Newsagent and ask them to order your books.

Please save me the following titles: Please tick | ✓ |

Title	Author	
A VERY STYLISH AFFAIR	*Emma Darcy*	
ELEMENT OF RISK	*Robyn Donald*	
TO HAVE AND TO HOLD	*Sally Wentworth*	
BURDEN OF INNOCENCE	*Patricia Wilson*	
LOVERS NOT FRIENDS	*Helen Brooks*	
THREADS OF DESTINY	*Sara Wood*	
INNOCENT DECEIVER	*Lilian Peake*	
WHISPER OF SCANDAL	*Kathryn Ross*	
CALYPSO'S ENCHANTMENT	*Kate Walker*	
SAVING THE DEVIL	*Sophie Weston*	
BETWEEN TWO LOVES	*Rosemary Hammond*	
DREAM MAN	*Quinn Wilder*	
STEP IN THE DARK	*Marjorie Lewty*	
LOVESTORM	*Jennifer Taylor*	
DECEPTIVE DESIRE	*Sally Carr*	
A PASSIONATE DECEIT	*Kate Proctor*	

If you would like to order these books in addition to your regular subscription from Mills & Boon Reader Service please send £1.90 per title to: Mills & Boon Reader Service, Freepost, P.O. Box 236, Croydon, Surrey, CR9 9EL, quote your Subscriber No:................................... (if applicable) and complete the name and address details below. Alternatively, these books are available from many local Newsagents including W H Smith, J Menzies, Martins and other paperback stockists from 9 December 1994.

Name:...

Address:..

....Post Code:...........................

To Retailer: If you would like to stock M&B books please contact your regular book/magazine wholesaler for details.

You may be mailed with offers from other reputable companies as a result of this application.
If you would rather not take advantage of these opportunities please tick box.   ☐